All I Want For Christmas Is A Cryptid

LIANA BROOKS

OTHER WORKS

ALL I WANT FOR CHRISTMAS

All I Want For Christmas Is A Werewolf
All I Want For Christmas Is A Reaper
All I Want For Christmas Is A Gargoyle
All I Want For Christmas Is A Cryptid

FLEET OF MALIK

Bodies In Motion
Change of Momentum

HEROES AND VILLAINS

Even Villains Fall In Love
Even Villains Go To The Movies
Even Villains Have Interns
Even Villains Play The Hero (omnibus)
The Polar Terror

TIME AND SHADOWS

The Day Before
Convergence Point
Decoherence

SHORTER WORKS

Darkness and Good
Escape: The Liana Brooks Sci Fi Collection
Fey Lights
If You Give A Skeleton A 3D Printer
Prime Sensations
The Complete Inklet Collection
The Price Of The Mountain Lily

Find other works by the author at www.lianabrooks.com

All I Want For Christmas Is A Cryptid

LIANA BROOKS

AUSTRALIA

Copyright © 2024 Liana Brooks

All rights reserved. No part of this book may be reproduced in any form or by any electronic or mechanical means, including information storage and retrieval systems, without permission in writing from the publisher, except by a reviewer, who may quote brief passages in a review.

This is a work of fiction. All characters, organisations and events are the author's creation, or are used fictitiously.

Paperback ISBN: 978-1-922434-99-9
Hardcover ISBN: 978-1-923305-00-7
eBook ISBN: 9798227646804

www.inkprintpress.com

National Library of Australia Cataloguing-in-Publication Data
Brooks, Liana 1982—
All I Want For Christmas Is A Cryptid
134 p.   cm.
ISBN: 978-1-922434-99-9
Inkprint Press, Canberra, Australia
1. Fiction—Romance—Paranormal—General 2. Fiction—Fantasy—Paranormal 3. Fiction—Holidays

Summary: Forcibly removed from her home as wildfires roll in, Phoebe must return to the life she left for dead eight years ago, complete with gold-diggers, celebrity smarm—and a spectacularly hot fireman.

First Edition: December 2024

Cover design © Inkprint Press
Bigfoot image © Dimuth Amarasiri via Pixabay.com

This book was published on Ngunnawal country. The publisher would like to acknowledge the people who have told their stories here for countless generations.

For everyone who has ever had to start over.

ALL I WANT FOR CHRISTMAS IS A CRYPTID

THERE WAS A KNOCK AT THE HEAVY WOODEN DOOR AT THE FRONT of the cabin. Clutching my pine-green blanket that warded off the winter chill, I closed the zombie book I was reading and leaned forward, nearly falling out of my oversized chair, and stared down the empty hall.

The cabin had no address.

There wasn't any indication there was a house out here except the wheel ruts left from my twice-monthly trip to the nearest town and the mail truck, if it was ever forced to come up here.

Everything ran on wind and solar power, what little there was to run. I didn't have cable, internet, or cellphone service here. I used solar box lamps in most rooms and the most entertainment I had was a flooded window well where, one spring, I'd had tadpoles.

Like everything else in my life, they'd gone away years ago.

The knock came again, shaking the frame of the old timber.

How bizarre.

I dropped my feet to the ground and shuffled over. For maybe the thirteenth time since I'd moved in, I wondered why the front door hadn't included a peephole. That would have been useful about now, or the other twelve times in eight years someone had knocked on the door unannounced.

Cautiously, I opened the door, struggling against the whine of the hinges. It was never locked, but that didn't matter because I never used the front door and it wasn't inclined to move for anything short of extreme force. I managed to get it open a crack to see someone standing on the dilapidated front porch, holding the broken screen door open. "You're not Angie."

Figured. Angie drove the mail truck and knew to come around back, or at least to the side patio.

The person in front of my door was tall, well past the six-foot height of the door and broad shouldered with a loose, blue flannel shirt over a well-washed gray tee. He had spring-green eyes, pushing towards an almost unnatural yellow, with shaggy brown hair and the start of a beard.

We made eye contact.

I leaned out the door just enough to look pointedly at the sign hanging at eye level:

- No, I won't sell the land.
- No, I won't sell the house.
- No, I won't buy anything.
- No, I don't want your religion.
- No, I don't want to be good neighbors.
- No, I don't know you.
- No, we're not long-lost cousins.
- No, I'm not that person you thought you knew.
- Yes, you should leave without knocking.

The sign was right where I'd left it.

It had taken me nearly a week of trial and error to create a resin pour over ink that I liked and that didn't ruin the paper, but it held. The answers to all the stranger's questions were clearly visible.

"¿No sabes leer inglés?" I asked in a flawless Mexico City accent.

"Happy holidays to you too, Sunshine. I read English just fine," the stranger said. His accent was pure Willamette Valley Oregonian with the teensiest suggestion of northern California.[1]

I looked, again, at the list.

The stranger narrowed his eyes. "I'm from the volunteer fire department. Are you David King?"

"No. He's dead. Is that all?"

My door was half-closed before a hand the size of my face stopped it. "Sorry, who are you?"

"Phoebe King. He left me the house when he died." I tapped my sign. "It's not for sale, et cetera, et cetera, et cetera. Goodbye."

"Phoebe?"

"Yes. Phoebe, the shining one," I said with a sigh. "Not to be confused with Phobos, the god of fear and panic, which would probably be a more appropriate name."

My would-be hero all but audibly blinked. "Do you always introduce yourself with a full story of your name?"

"No. Generally I don't speak to anyone at all, but you seemed to want a conversation."

"Actually, I'm here from the fire depart—"

Right. I held up a finger, stepped back inside, and turned the corner into the tiny front room, possibly meant as a coat room, where I kept mail and documents. The fire department one was in the red folder next to the dead hedgehog cactus in the red clay pot with a firebird on it.

Returning with the slip of paper, I held it out to the man.

---

[1] Before life in the cabin I'd sat through a lot of linguistics, amongst other things, although knowing where his accent was from admittedly wasn't particularly helpful.

"What's this?" He stared at it in bewilderment.

"You said you could read English! The answer is there, in black and white with my signature in blue pen. I talked to your fire chief. I understand that if my house burns down I will have to pay out of pocket. I told the chief to let the house burn. If I'm in it, so be it. This is the legal form clearing the department of all wrongdoing. Go away."

A large foot got between the door and the door frame as I tried to push it shut.

Through the gap, I glared at the intruder. "Whatever the question is, the answer is no. Go away."

"Listen, there's a wildfire coming, you should evacuate."

"No." I'd noticed the air smelled a little smoky this morning, but I figured it was someone warming their house with a woodfire somewhere across the valley.

"The fire is out of control and swinging this way, there's a shelter forty miles down the highway."

"I only go as far as Fair Oaks."

"Fair Oaks is evacuating."

"Right. Hold on." I scurried back to my document shelf and pulled out the DNR,[2] the will leaving everything here to Iris Muhly[3] or the charity of her choosing, and a copy of the phrase *Go Away And Leave Me Alone* written in every language I knew.[4]

When I turned around, the man was standing in the doorway.

I blinked. I didn't even know the door could open that wide.

---

[2] Do Not Resuscitate—if I became severely incapacitated, I wasn't coming back again. Once was enough.

[3] I'd never talked to her, but I saw an interview she did once that was broadcast to the diner in Fair Oaks and something about her seemed as lost and lonely as I was, so I figured she'd enjoy the randomness of the gift.

[4] Except ASL—I couldn't draw the signs—but 23 out of 24 isn't bad.

He scowled.

"Here." I handed him the papers. "Go away."

He folded the papers in half, and then in half again, pressing the creases down neatly before tucking them into his back pocket. "You got a suitcase, lady?"

"No."

"Bags?"

"No. I came up here for a daytrip."

"When was that?"

"Eight years, four months, and three days ago. It was a Wednesday in late May. The wildflowers were in bloom and there were bees trying to turn the grill into a hive. I had to stay late, to clean it up." I could still smell the honeysuckle and clean wind, hear the buzz of the bees and the silence, the great, engulfing silence that drowned out all my screams.

Even more important, nothing up here beeped.

I'd go mad if I had to listen to another clock ticking away the seconds between life and death, another monitor beeping as something failed.

The man was staring in horror now, eyebrows punched together and raised, lips pressed in a moue of concern.

Looking around at the nothingness that filled the empty front hall, I clicked my tongue, nodded, and held a hand out to the door in the classic Midwestern gesture that said, "Please leave before I get my shotgun."

The stranger probably misinterpreted it because he was from the west coast, where, apparently, someone pointing at the open door meant, "Please come in and sit a spell."

He walked right in, down the long, dusty hallway into the green space where I'd spent most of my life for the past eight years.

The eastern wall was stained glass, a chaotic medley of colors depicting a fairy forest. My first winter at the cabin the wall there had been too thin, and cold air had seeped in like the breath of death, so I'd gone to the workshop and done the best I could with what I had. The following autumn I'd welded hooks to the thick, black iron lines between the glass so vines could grow along it. I had the classic spider plant,[5] but thornless blackberries and thick pomegranates too, winding up the walls around the room.

Their roots were planted on the north wall with the window that flooded each spring and sometimes had tadpoles. There had been a hole in the cabin wall and the plants from the outside garden were coming in. Killing them all was unthinkable, so I'd extended the walls, added a woodfire oven-and-sometimes-kiln and a solar oven, and put roofing where it was needed to keep the wind out.

The flooded window, now dingy and dry, looked into the overgrown courtyard where in the fall the leaves rustled bright October orange. At this time of year, though, the skeletal branches reached for the unforgiving sky, silently pleading for spring and a new chance at life.

The cabin's west wall curved outwards, with a huge bench meant for giants stuffed with green and purple pillows, narrow shelves filled with books and rocks between the five arched windows that stretched up into the darkness of the cathedral ceiling, and piles of abandoned projects. Embroidery. Knitting. Hand sewing. Journals. Recipe books.

Somewhere in there I was pretty sure was a mortar and pestle with the dried mountain blueberries I was crushing for ink.

If the stranger had looked up, he would have seen the rope ladder that went up to the second floor and the loft where more pillows made a bed[6] and a telescope looked

---

[5] *Chlorophytum comosum.*
[6] Getting a mattress and bedframe delivered and set up upstairs had been too overwhelming, so I'd skipped it.

out over the mountains and foothills to the south.

There were stairs, but they were at the front of the house by the old kitchen and the office I'd come to clear out.

As soon as the office was done, I could go.

But I'd have to drive on a highway to leave, and I couldn't do that.

So I stayed.

I'd stayed so long that even the thought of leaving had faded away.

Sometimes I remembered I was supposed to go back to the life I'd had.

There were papers that needed reviewing. Editors who wanted meetings. People who wanted to talk to me. Questions I would be expected to answer.

If I could find a way to drive on the highway, I'd go back to all that.

But I couldn't. The office needed cleaning, and I hadn't done that yet.

Besides, there was still food in the fridge, and the plants needed watering.

It wasn't time to leave yet.

The bewildered man loomed in the tiny forest of my living space like a young redwood. He turned, looking back at the empty hall.

I turned too, looking at the wasted space. The hall curved a bit so the colors of the back rooms were hidden from view.

"This place looks abandoned from out front."

"It is, mostly," I said. "It's only me."

"We only knew there was someone up here because the post office had you listed." Somehow his wide, green eyes went wider. "Tell me you at least have a gun."

"No."

He closed his eyes and probably swore under his breath. "This is bear country."

"I have bear spray. It works on bears and humans. Shall I go get it?"

"Shall you?" The corner of his mouth lifted in a broken smile. "Who talks like that?"

"Me." I looked again at the open front door. "I thought that was obvious. Like my desire for you to leave."

"We are leaving." He nodded.

"We as in the Royal We? Or We as in the Fire Department We?" I sat back on my oversized chair under the rope ladder and pulled my legs under the blanket.

"We as in You and Me."

I shook my head. "There is no You And Me. There's You, who is leaving. There's Me, who is staying."

"There's a wildfire."

"So you said."

"You could die."

I stared politely at him as I waited for him to make a point.

"Burning to death is a terrible way to go."

"I'd suffocate in under ten minutes."

"That's a long time."

I leaned forward. "Seven years is a long time. Sixty hours is a long time. Ten minutes?" I shook my head as I shrugged and settled back into my chair. "I've been dead for longer than that."

In case he didn't get the hint, I picked up the book I'd been reading, a silly one with a bright pink cover.

"Where's your room?" the man asked.

I glanced up the rope ladder.

"Do you have suitcases?"

I shook my head as I turned the page. I knew I shouldn't encourage him, but the stranger seemed insistent on having this wholly unnecessary conversation.

"Fine." He grabbed one of the woven baskets overflowing with blankets and fluffy socks from by the bay window. "Put your stuff in here and let's go."

"No." I turned another page and snuggled in under my blanket. Truly, dealing with people was exhausting. That's why I never did it anymore.

"I'm not leaving you here to die."

"Why not?"

"I don't want ghosts haunting the mountains!"

The answer was so ludicrous I actually looked up. The stranger was only a few steps away, face lit by the fairy colors of the stained glass, almost a ghost himself.

I closed my book because I couldn't let a decent plot be ruined by hearing this conversation. "You do realize there is no scientific evidence for ghosts. They don't exist. When a person dies, their body decays. Time breaks down cell walls, leeches all the marrow from the bone, and eventually reduces the body to nothing but the hard calcium deposits and any plastic or metal inserts you might have had. All that's left is a fading memory of a person."

The man's strange eyes went wide again. "There's something wrong with you."

"Multiple things, actually." I smiled and opened my book again. "Can you close the door, the air quality isn't improving."

He stalked off and the door slammed shut.

I breathed a sigh of relief, reopened my book, and folded myself all the way under my heavy blanket so it covered my head.

Curse all the gods and monsters in the world. Every single fictional superbeing that manipulated fates and destinies. I hated them all, individually and collectively.

If there was some supreme being weaving my fate, I was going to find their scissors and gouge their eye out.

How dare they threaten me again?

How dare they?

After all I'd done. After all I'd lost.

I was safe here, with my overgrown garden and well water, my solar lamps and wind generator. I had good books and gorgeous views. I had silence.

Sweet, blessed, beautiful silence.

My ears drank in the emptiness free of sirens, ticking tocks, and beeps.

There was an unusual rustle of fabric.

Light pierced the shadowed gloom of my fortress as someone lifted the blanket just a enough for eyes green as the spider plant's leaves to stare at me.

"You were supposed to be on the other side of the door when you shut it."

"I know."

"You can go out the side door if you want."

"Okay, but only if you come with."

"No."

"Why not?"

"My mother told me never to take rides from strangers."

"I'm not a stranger."

"I don't know your name. That makes you a stranger."

"Adam," he said and I tried to place it. "Adam Sandlake. We talked at the hardware store last month? You were looking for pliers?"

Pliers? There was a vague recollection of a trip to the store, and a strange man looming over me who asked what I wanted, and I'd gone with the first thing I saw just to escape the situation.

"And you're Phoebe?" Adam asked. "The post office says the house belongs to a David?"

"David's my father. This is his cabin. He used to come here on the weekends away from mom."

"Did they fight a lot?"

"She was dying and caregiving someone is emotionally draining, so he took every other weekend to come out here and take care of his mental health. His office and workshop are here. I came to clean them out." I sat up, letting the blanket fall down around my waist. This was the same response I'd given to every therapist for sixteen years. I could recite it without a single tear. "She died when I was seventeen, just after my graduation."

"You graduated high school at seventeen?"

"College. I was precocious."

"Okay, so, is your dad not coming up any more?"

"He died eight years ago, on the way to a book launch."

Adam nodded slowly. "And you've been here, almost since he died?"

"I came up as soon as I left the hospital."

His eyes slanted sideways as he did the math. "How long were you in the hospital?"

"Long enough."

"Okay. Do you have any other family? Siblings? Cousins?"

"No."

"Friends? Exes?"

"No."

"If you die, will anyone notice?"

"Of course. I left a copy of my will with you, my family lawyer has one on file, and so does my university, my editor, and my agent."

His brows furrowed in perplexion. "Do you think any of those people want to see you again?"

"No."

"No?"

"They get paid either way."

"Right." He reached into his pocket and pulled out a cellphone with a black cover and a white outline of Bigfoot along with the words *World Hide And Seek Champion*. "Here, take this."

"There's no reception out here." I took the phone that was the size of my hand and stared at it. I didn't even recognize the brand.

"Don't worry, you can use it to call your lawyer when we get to town."

"I'm not going to tow—"

Adam stood, scooping me and my blanket up with him. "Yes, you are. I'm taking you. To town. By any means necessary."

"You can't do that!" I hit his shoulder as hard as I could. It was like hitting a boulder.

"I can. Because I'm going to say you were showing signs of delirium, possibly from smoke inhalation, and I rescued you."

Twisting, I threw myself out of his arms, grabbed the rope ladder, and hauled myself up to the loft where I threw the first thing I could find at him.

Adam dodged as the pot rolled. "Did you just throw a cactus at me?"

"Yes!"

"You *can* say yes!" His expression was altogether alien and strange, the glimmer of a sidhe[7] lord's smile mixed with an alley cat's cunning. "Get any clothes you need while you're up there, and a bag if you have one. We're leaving in five."

"Why are we rushing?"

"It's eleven in the morning," he said, pointing at the stained glass window. It was noticeably darker than it had been a few minutes before.

As if to add emphasis, the solar lamp by my pillows flickered to life.

"The fire is moving fast, we have to outrun the smoke. Get your stuff. Get anything you can't replace. We are leaving in four and a half minutes."

---

[7] It's Irish. It's pronounced "She". They're the shining ones, the good folk, the "good" fairies. You still wouldn't want to cross one.

I didn't own much. I never had.

When I was little I had a room that looked like a fairy princess's, all gold and purple and pink with my father's stained glass and my mother's math-based fractal landscapes painted in watercolor. I could remember the colors, the view of the Hemiciclo A Juarez[8] from our front window, and the smell of enchiladas and chilies in the air. I probably had clothes, since I was fairly certain most children did, but all I remembered was the colors and the smells.

By the time I was a teen, I had books and classes. Mom had doctor's appointments. Dad had a busy schedule.

We downsized, sold the house, moved out west to be near mom's cousins and the doctors she needed. We kept downsizing. Until it was the one-room apartment and the cabin Tito Pedro left Mom in his will. I slept in the apartment at night while Dad stayed in the hospital with Mom. In the mornings I ate breakfast and switched places, taking my classes online by her side as the machines beeped and nurses hurried in and out on their daily rounds.

Now, somehow, I owned less.

The washing machine I had was powered by hand crank or bicycle, and it only held about four outfits. All of which I stuffed into a gray duffle bag with the word NO embroidered on it. I dropped it over the edge of the loft as the smoke smell became more pronounced.

---

[8] It's a marble monument on the south side of Alameda Central Park near Alameda Barrio in Mexico City.

"Is that everything?" Adam asked.

Common sense was apparently not available to the man. Anyone else would have realized that dying to save me was pointless and they should have hightailed it out of here when they saw the sign at my door.

"I need to go to the office. It's what I came here to do." I climbed down the ladder, Adam's phone knocking against my hip in the pocket of my tea-length juniper skirt. Once I was down, I took out the phone and took pictures of the house with the fairy lights and solar lamps on. I had good pictures of the stained glass already preserved offsite, but I took another picture with the vines and berries, just in case the fire came this far.

"Where's the office?"

"Down the second hall."

Adam stared at me like I'd lost my mind.

Well, maybe he had a point. With a sigh I pulled vines away from the door, fished under some blankets for the door handle, and opened the narrow door to the other half of the house. Technically, it could be reached from the document room up front, but the roof on the kitchen wasn't stable enough that I'd use it.

My feet became almost too heavy to move. This hall, *this hall* was the last untouched space. The last place my father had written. The last place with my mother's unfinished art. The last place I needed to take care of before I could transition to life without anyone.

"It's getting warm," Adam said behind me. "We need to go or we're going to get trapped in here."

I shook my head. "I can't. I... I..." Stepping back, I breathed in smoky, warm air and wondered how long it would take to suffocate.

"What do you need from there?"

"The laptop. Hard drive. Painting. Files." I knew the list by heart. Originally it had been on my phone in the notes app. When the phone started dying, I'd transferred it to a physical note; the paper was probably still around here somewhere.

I turned, drinking in the sight of my safe and shaded living space.

There was noise behind me, footsteps walking away, and they sounded so odd but they fit the time of my racing heartbeat.

What I needed, what I really needed, was... "Water," I decided out loud.

A drink of water and I could go back to reading. Maybe I'd meditate first. Close my eyes and just detach from everything for a little bit.

The footsteps returned, angry and heavy, and stormed past me like life always did.

The front door opened with a creak, slammed shut.
Reopened.

Turning with a frown, I saw Adam approaching with a determined glint in his green eyes.

Before I could object to the way he kept walking into my house, he was in front of me, picking me up and dumping me over one shoulder.

"Time to go." He grabbed my baskets with his free hand and stole me away.

"Put me down!" I managed to hit one of his swinging hips as the front porch steps threatened to give me a concussion. "I do not consent to this!"

"Hold your horses, I'm putting you down." He plunked me into the front seat of either a truck that was new in 1980 or a newer model built to look like something built in 1980. "Stay," he ordered.

"I'm not a dog!" I pushed his hand away as he tried to buckle me in.

His eyes met mine and they were filled with fury. "I know. Dogs have the common sense to run away from forest fires!"

"I—!"

Didn't have a cogent counter to that.

There was smoke boiling over the hillside burning my eyes already.

"Fine." Taking the seatbelt, I secured myself.

Adam slammed my door, tossed the baskets in the truck bed, and climbed into the driver's seat.

"I'll go as far as Fair Oaks. If you drop me there I'll be fine."

"Fair Oaks evacuated," he said as the truck careened down the rubble drive towards the main dirt road. "I told you that already."

Panic stole all reason. I shut my eyes. "I don't know what's past Fair Oaks. Is there a—a community center? Campground? Something?"

"We'll head to Sutherlin. We can catch five from there."

"Five? As in I-5? The highway?" I looked out at the smoky landscape. "I'd rather die."

"You don't—" He stopped talking when he looked at me. "Did you have medicines you need?"

"No."

"Did you eat today?"

"Yes."

"It's just…" There was a telling pause. "You don't look so good."

"Possibly because I was kidnapped by a strange man, my home is under threat of being burned to ash, and I'm currently homeless," I asked in a tight voice. I was trying to rise above the stress, I truly was, but I was well past my limits. "That's a lot of stress for one day."

"I didn't kidnap you. I rescued you."

"I'm not a princess. I don't need rescuing."

"Everyone needs rescuing sometimes."

Perhaps, but I didn't have to admit it. Instead, I stared out the window and sulked. I'd left my book on the couch too.

Ugh.

Closing my eyes, I tried to sleep. In nightmares, that always worked. I fell asleep in the dream and woke up on my couch. All I wanted was to wake up safe, at home, protected by the sturdy barriers of untouched memories.

I must have dozed, because I woke to the sound of voices and the smell of charcoal.

The truck jerked to a stop and Adam cursed under his breath. "Everyone and his dog is here."

Sitting up, I looked around at a church parking lot filled with campers, cars, fire trucks, and grills stuffed with food trying to feed the hungry masses. My stomach turned. There were hundreds of people out there. "Why are we here?"

"The Bi-Mart lot was full. This is rendezvous point six."

There were six of these nightmares? "Do we need to be here?"

"I need to check in and figure out what's happening. The Whistler's Bend fire is curving north, but the Kanipe fire is moving south. All the dry grass in the fields is hurting us. It's been too dry this autumn."

Only half those words made sense to me. Whistler's Bend was south of North Umpqua River, I knew that much. It wasn't likely to run dry, even during a drought, but it was narrow enough that a high wind could take sparks and ash across. It'd been a dry year, with the lack of rain being a main talking point of every casual conversation I'd had since February.[9]

Kanipe I only knew as a campsite north of home, I'd never gone. But the implication that we were caught between two fires didn't bode well for anyone.

The midday sky was a hazy gray.

Adam unbuckled and looked around, clicking his tongue. "Okay, do you want to get out?"

---

[9] There'd been maybe nine conversations in the past ten months. Maybe.

"No." With all my heart I wished I would wake up back at home.

My would-be rescuer opened his mouth as if to say something and then stopped. He reached out, placing his hand next to mine on the seat. "I get it, you're not a people person."

"Not for many years," I confirmed.

"I know it was hard leaving your house. I know you want to get home."

I nodded, but I didn't know where he was going with this speech.

"I'll stick with you, okay? Until you're safe and settled. Will that help?"

The thought turned over in my mind for a moment, then I nodded again. "Yes. That seems fair. You decided to drag me away, you get to be responsible for keeping me alive."

He laughed. "You have a weird way of looking at things."

"If you missed the red flags, that's a You Problem. I've been nothing but honest about what I wanted."

"Sure." He laughed. "It's all my fault. You want some food? I don't know if they have vegetarian."

"I can eat whatever," I said, because as much as I wanted to ignore reality, my stomach was grumbling, and dying of starvation was not on my list of acceptable outcomes.

With a nod, Adam got out of the truck and left me alone. But he took the keys, the bastard.

I took a deep breath, looked out at the burning world. So... Here I was. Back in the land of the living. Interacting with people. Partaking in civilization.

I hated it.

In the end, Adam volunteered to go further south since his truck could still drive and families were being prioritized at rendezvous points one through six. I ate a couple of hot dogs, had a can of West Coast Cola that was flatter than Kansas and tasted of dishwater, and then we were off, winding through the backroads of Oregon as the radio played.

I didn't often tune into world events, or, really, the world. After twenty minutes of the radio, it sounded like I had missed a minor apocalypse or three. There was a severe economic downturn,[10] droughts across the country,[11] and war on almost every major continent.[12]

While I suffered through the highlight reel of tragedy, Adam loomed like the specter of death in the driver's seat. A part of me that spoke with my mother's Chilango accent insisted I should play nice, ask him questions, get him to open up.

Memories of phone calls with police sirens in the background drowned out her advice.

Adam shifted in his seat as the news cycled and he hit the button to turn the radio off. "So, Phoebe, what do you do all day?"

"Avoid humanity." I crossed my arms and glowered at the road in front of us.

---

[10] Again.
[11] Again.
[12] Congrats to Antarctica and Australia I guess?

"I'll consider myself special then."

"Don't. I'm only talking to you because there is no polite way to ignore you when you've dragged me bodily from my home and across the state."

"At least you're being polite about it," he said with a sigh.

"You fed me."

He glanced at me, eyebrows knotted and mouth caught in an open frown as if the words were stuck in his mouth.

"Apologies," I said, hugging my new[13] black backpack that I'd found in the basket in the truck bed to my chest, "my social skills are severely atrophied."

"But your vocabulary is fantastic."

"It should be, I have a doctorate in linguistics and I was the youngest member of the new dictionary team."

I did some mental math and was dismayed to realize I'd last contributed to the team over twelve years ago, when I was still in my teens and working on my first doctorate. It probably wasn't even in the headlines anymore.

Story of my life, really. Everything I'd ever done, every project I'd poured my heart and soul into, had dried to dust and blown away in the wind, forgotten by everyone but me. Over the years, I supposed I'd been forgotten too.

No family. No friends. No career. No contact with anyone. In every way but the physical, I was dead.

But alive enough to want to keep living. That was something to mull over when I had a moment.

I could have stayed in the path of the fire. I could have run into it with open arms.

I didn't.

Maybe that meant something.

That was a worry I ruthlessly shoved aside. "What about you?"

---

[13] 'Stolen' might be a more accurate term.

"I usually work the forestry service on a seasonal basis. Do you work, or are you a live-off-the-land type?"

"I had a job, but I took some time off. The house doesn't need much, and I get deliveries if I need something I don't have. Books, mostly." I tucked my feet up on the seat and watched the world roll by, winter-brown hills and distant peaks pining for snow.

"Family?"

"Dead."

"Sorry to hear that."

I shrugged. "You probably didn't kill them."

It occurred to me that it would be weird if he had been the drunk driver who'd ended my father's life, but it was statistically unlikely, and I was fairly certain the police report said the driver was an older gentleman. Adam didn't look old enough to be considered old.

The comment still earned me another odd look.

I offered him a little facial shrug. It was the truth, after all; he probably wasn't the reason I was all alone. There'd been a trial, and I'd planned to go, but I needed to get things from the house. Retrieve the laptop. Tidy up. I just hadn't been able to get it all done in time.

"Here's our stop," Adam said as a faded wooden sign welcomed us to another small town. "If they don't have somewhere here for you, we can try northern Cali. They're opening up a few hotels for refugees."

"I'm not a refugee. I'm an abductee."

"Yeah, I'm sure there's a sheriff around here. You can tell 'em about how the big, burly mountain man forced you to not die in the raging wildfire. I'm sure they can find a nice mental health ward for you."

"That's a vicious threat," I said as we pulled into the parking lot of what was, according to the signage, the community center.

"What's a threat?"

"Threatening to lock me up for mental instability."

He sighed again, eyes closing in what was perhaps a prayer, but was probably a curse. "Listen, you wanted to stay and burn. That's not a healthy thought for anyone. Burning to death, suffocating in a wildfire, that's not a quick death. It's not a good one. And I get why you're stressed about driving—"

"You really don't."

"—but leaving you there wasn't an option. We're here now. We'll find you a safe place. I'd like to do that as a team, not under threat of being reported for a crime I definitely didn't commit. Okay?"

My eyes narrowed. "I suppose, from your point of view, I was being the teensiest bit irrational."

"Just the teensiest," he agreed.

"I'll endeavor to be more rational if that helps. Maybe think like a man." I managed to cut an entire tirade before I spit acid.

The corner of Adam's mouth lifted in a suppressed smile. "The smartest person in this car is a lady, so probably no need to think like a man," he said with only a hint of mountain drawl, "but if we could be friends, I'd like that. I promised I'd help you get somewhere safe, and I meant it. I'll get you somewhere safe and then I'll be out of your hair. Okay?"

"You're going to keep me safe?"

"That's what I said."

Slowly, I nodded. "Fine."

"Friends?" He held out his hand.

"Friends," I agreed, and we shook hands like we were five. Although, if memory served, the person I'd attempted to befriend at age five had been a professor emeritus. But I had been invited to her 90th birthday party, or at least my parents had, and I'd gotten it into my head that going to someone's birthday party made us friends.

By that logic, I'd have to ask Adam his birthday and see if I was supposed to mail him a present. Hopefully he liked books; it certainly didn't look like we had the same fashion tastes.

He hopped out and walked around the truck to open my door.

I climbed out into smoke-choked air and followed him past the full parking lot through a narrow glass door to a large, linoleum-tiled room with lunch-room tables spread out and a row of mismatched crockpots lining the low stage.

A few weary-looking people glanced at us as we walked in, but most were focused on the big TV on the far end of the room where the news was playing.

Maps of four major wildfires across the state were on display next to a quote from the president about a state of emergency in the Pacific Northwest.

Circling the edge of the room, I carefully approached the hastily assembled snack table filled with the most random assortment of back-of-the-cupboard abandoned items past their Best By date. Some of the granola bars were from a company that had gone bankrupt before my father died, and at least half the fruit was moldy.

I grabbed an apple that looked okayish and made a mental note to send the town an anonymous check to help resupply their emergency stores when I had a moment. Which, looking at the fire maps, did not look like it would be soon. While I'd been spending the colder months curled up with a good book, the state of Oregon had been turning itself into a crispy, dry tinderbox ready to explode at the first spark on the highway.

The relentless slog of misery and dire predictions was interrupted by whimsical music as the faces of a devastatingly handsome man and equally beautiful woman appeared wearing the most shimmery fantasy armor I'd seen in years.

Granted, I didn't watch much television, but this looked like something pulled straight from my teenage imagination. Several scenes played out across the screen, epic battles and looks filled with longing and loathing. Then the words "Who Should Die?" flashed on the screen with a list of names.

Familiar names.

Valiant Verrat. Wysha.[14] Mempha. Zjarr Aabo. Pameta. Devana. Akull.

My heart stopped in my chest.

This was *really* plucked from my imagination.

This was *my* book. The one I'd written with my father.

He'd told me there was some big news about a television show, but we'd never discussed it in detail. It did explain where the extra money in my bank account had come from though. I mean, sales were lovely, but book sales didn't traditionally make one wealthy to the point where they could retire at age twenty-two. I'd simply dismissed it as an extra annuity from my parents' accounts, but it looked like the books I'd written were quite popular.[15]

My father had been a professor of economics, amongst other things; there was no way he hadn't written a deal that didn't profit us significantly.

Adam walked over, sipping hot chocolate mix almost stirred into water. "Do you know about this?"

"I'm familiar with the series," I hedged. "Why is Wysha on the chopping block? She's alive at the end of the series."

"At the end of book four, sure," Adam agreed. "But no one knows what's in book five. Vegas odds have her dead

---

[14] This was the show Iris Muhly was working on?!
[15] I admit, looking back, there were a number of red flags for depression. I should have reached out. I should have cared. But one of the things about depression is you don't care, and you don't realize until later how much you didn't care. It's not all tears and rage, sometimes it's simply an emptiness. I couldn't summon the will to care, so I hadn't. And there'd been no one else to pick up the pieces.

by chapter two. What do you think?"

My mouth went dry. "I wouldn't bet on it."

Adam shrugged. "Even money, I'd say."

The commercials ended and another map of wildfires in the Pacific Northwest filled the screen.

"The hotels are filled up around here," Adam said, "but they're saying there are rooms free about an hour south, down in Cali. Is that okay? Do you need anything before we go?"

"I need to make a phone call, but it can wait until morning."

Books five and six were in my bag and suddenly, for the first time in years, I had a desperate need to get them to my editor.

My favorite character's life was at stake.

We'd driven halfway to Redding[16] before we finally found an exit that wasn't guarded by highway patrol waving people fleeing the fire on past packed hotels. For the first time in eight years, I wished I had a cellphone so I could see how bad the disaster really was. How much of Oregon had to be on fire for us to need to go this far south?

Adam pulled into a fueling station, attached the truck to the recharger, and leaned into the rolled-down window. "I'm going to go in, see if we can find a hotel near here."

An ambulance screamed past behind us.

"Can we stay somewhere else?" I asked. "Maybe find somewhere further away from the hospital and traffic?"

"I'll ask and see if anyone knows of a place, but it's probably slim pickings. I'll get you some earplugs though. That'll help."

It most certainly would not help, but I would let him pretend. While he walked away, I took inventory of my life: a box of papers, an old laptop stuffed in the black backpack with my mother's last painting wrapped in an old flannel next to it, and a handwoven wicker picnic basket holding all my clothes. All I'd grabbed otherwise was my purse—the one shaped like a book, naturally—that had my driver's license, passport, and a bank card that expired in a month. I had a whole thirty cents to my name in cash.

---

[16] Still nine hours from L.A.

That was not going to get me very far.

Adam came back with two bottles of water and a reusable bag full of chips and instant ramen packs.

I raised my eyebrows in confusion.

"Dinner might be hard to get. There's smoke over in McCloud and everyone's nervous."

"I have no idea where that is."

"East of here."

Opening the water bottle, I tried to find some focus other than the threat of smoke inhalation or burning to death as Adam started driving again. "Can I borrow your phone?"

"Sure. You know someone around here? I can drop you off."

"All my California contacts live near Los Angeles." A place I was dearly hoping to avoid. I thumbed open Adam's phone and looked at the moody picture of Oregon's rugged coastline. "Nice picture."

"Thanks. I took it myself."

Dialing a number from memory, I only belatedly looked at the time. Past eight in the evening in late December. Was that still working hours in L.A.?

"Hey!" A female voice that was both familiar and not answered when I was one ring from hanging up. "You got Jeanie, who's this?"

"It's Phoebe," I said, trying not to choke on my own name, "Phoebe King. David's daughter."

Silence stretched on the phone for an uncomfortable moment. "Holy ducks in water!" Jeanie didn't quite swear. "I thought you were dead!"

"Yeah, I can understand that."

Adam shot me a look with a furrowed brow.

I shook off his unspoken question with a shake of my head. "I've been up at the cabin."

"This whole time?" Jeanie demanded.

"Yes." I licked my lips. Why was this so hard? "Um, about the books."

"Do you have the last one?"

"I have the last two."

Despite all expectations, the world did not screech to a halt with this news. The stars didn't fall. The sun didn't rise in the west. The world didn't actually tilt off its axis despite my earth shattering, or *Shattered*-shattering, news.

"Fabulous!" Jeanie said without any change in inflection. "When will you have them in to me?"

Adam was pulling into the parking lot of a three-story hotel. "Sit tight, I'm going to check us in."

"I should be settled in an hour," I told Jeanie as Adam walked out of sight. "I'm near Redding right now. There's wildfires."

"Isn't it wild? I've been watching the news and we've got the smoke here! I'm glad you're safe though. Send me the manuscripts. I'll skim them tomorrow and get them to the editor, oh, let's say January? Maybe February. Let's not rush this."

"What about the TV show vote?" I asked as I stepped out of the car, stretching and looking around. There was a hospital less than a block away. A lost pink flipflop sitting under a berry-pink VW Bug. The charging cord for the truck hanging out of the front end... Little reminders everywhere that I wasn't home.

"The TV show?" Jeanie asked with a tone of voice that suggested she'd really rather not discuss it at all. "You saw that?"

"Yeah, when we stopped to find a place for lunch." I popped the hood of the truck to roll the charging cord up, phone pressed between my ear and shoulder. "My dad mentioned the show before he died, but I don't remember the details. He didn't even make it sound like a sure thing. Can you send me a copy of the contract?"

"Sure!"

"And stop the vote." The truck hood slammed down. "Wysha doesn't die."

There was another stretched silence on the other end. "Jeanie?"

"Only the first four books are under contract," she started.

"There is no way in hell my father signed the contract giving the show runners the rights to our intellectual property. Those characters, that world, all of it is mine. I wrote books five and six myself. Unless the showrunners are ending the show at the end of book four, they can't do anything more. If they want to have a season five, they'll need my approval, and they won't get that if this vote goes through and they kill off the wrong character. You need to call them and call off the vote."

As I turned from glaring at myself in the tinted window of the truck, I saw Adam standing behind me looking mildly concerned about my tone of voice.

A half-forgotten emotion crawled across my skin. "Sorry," I told Jeanie.

She took a deep breath. "No! No. It's not a worry. I just, it's late, you know? This is a lot to rush through. I really wish you'd called a few months ago."

"I hadn't planned on coming back to civilization a few months ago." Which begged a very uncomfortable question... "When were you planning on contacting me about all of this?"

"I did try calling you."

"I sent you a letter several years ago telling you my phone was broken. You could have mailed me something at any point."

"It's so inefficient."

"It's more efficient than not telling me what was going on."

Adam stood next to me. "Everything okay?"

I shook my head no.

"It's late," Jeanie said. "Why don't you go settle in wherever it is you are. Email me the manuscripts. And tomorrow you can go get a phone and we'll have a proper conversation looking at the options. I know you want the TV show to stay true to your work, but let me do my job first. The vote might not be a bad thing."

"Fine. I'll call you tomorrow once I have my own phone."

"Talk to you then." Jeanie closed the call with a click.

Dropping the phone into the basket Adam held out to me, I ground my teeth together. I felt gross, the pockets of my skirt were heavy, the air quality was terrible, everything smelled like burning pine, and my stomach was turning. I'd thought it would take actual brain trauma to make me want to go into a hotel, but for right now I could almost stomach the thought.

I trudged after Adam, letting his chatter fall around me like forgotten leaves.

There was a lobby: it looked the same as every midlist hotel lobby in existence, convenient shades of brown and beige with a fake plant in the corner.

We took the elevator up: it smelled of sweat, spilled beer, and bad perfume.

We trudged to a corner room on the third floor.

Adam opened the door into a small entryway with a closet, a doorway to a bathroom, and the hotel bedroom with a very obvious flaw.

I blinked. The universe delighted in mocking me today, and this was no exception. "There's only one bed."

I LOOKED BACK AT ADAM AND THE SINGLE HOTEL KEYCARD HE WAS holding.

"There's only one room," he said, holding out the key.

I took it and tried to wrap my tongue around the correct words. Adam was tall, handsome, conventionally attractive in that west coast way that meant he grunged up good. If I were looking for a relationship, he might have been my type, but I wasn't looking.

"I…" I licked my lips and tried to find words. "I mean, you're obviously quite physically appealing."

Adam half-laughed, cheeks turning pink as he looked away, running a hand through his hair.

"But I barely know you. And I'm really not in a good place to start a relationship."

"There's only one bed because only one person is staying. I'm gone," Adam said with a smile.

My long neglected libido was replaced by a far-more-familiar burning rage.

The world collapsed into ash and forgotten dreams.

I was being abandoned.

Again.

"You're leaving me? Why?" My breath caught in my throat, choking me as surely as the wildfire smoke would have.

Outside, sirens screamed in the busy city.

Adam stared at me for a long moment as if he thought I was crazy. Finally, he shook his head, dismissing the conversation. "Because I need to go back home."

"Are you going to the fire line?" That almost made sense. It was forgivable, at the very least. The fire line needed people.

"No. The state's sending wildfire crews out to handle it. They earn the good money. I'm just a local volunteer. I'll head home and won't go back out unless they need a backcountry guide."

"Take me with you."

"To my place? You don't want to go there, it's in the middle of nowhere."

I rolled my eyes. "To my home, thank you very much. The one you dragged me out of against my will."

"Listen," he sighed, "I looked at the map. Your property is behind the fire line. Until the fire is checked and someone gives the go-ahead to head back, you can't go home."

"How long until that happens?"

"A week, if you're lucky and anything is still standing. That fire burned hot and I'm not sure there will be much left. Insurance adjusters will probably come out in a couple of weeks—"

"Weeks?" Weeks trapped in this hell of a city alone? Untenable.

"It's the end of the year. People are gone for the holidays."

"What am I supposed to do? Stay here?"

Adam nodded. "The room's reserved for the next week. The county or state'll pay for it. All you need is to email your receipt in to the state wildfire website. They'll cut you a check to reimburse you."

"But you get to go home? How is that fair?" My fingers tightened around the basket handle, squeezing wood until it creaked in protest.

"It's not, but the fire wasn't on my end of the county."

"You can't just leave me here! How—what—no!" I all but stomped my foot, an overgrown toddler ready to throw a tantrum. "I don't want to be here, and I am, because of you."

He nodded again. "Yup. Life's unfair. You're welcome for saving you."

"You're very much not thanked," I said, shaking with rage. In another minute I was going to be in tears and the last thing I needed was for this would-be hero to laugh at me as I sobbed.

"You're tired," Adam said. "You're upset. I get that. Tomorrow morning you're going to wake up, the day will be better, and you won't even think of me."

"You promised me that you'd stay with me." I tried to keep the emotion out of my voice so he'd understand I was being rational. "That you'd be responsible for me until I was safe."

"I kept my promise. You're safe. You can take care of yourself from here."

Choking on the thick city air, I managed to drag myself to the door and open it. "Out of respect for everyone else in the hotel, I won't slam the door."

"Have a goodnight." Adam waved as he walked away.

"Let me know if you change your mind," I said as politely as possible.

"Won't happen," he said as the elevator dinged.

I shuddered, shut my door as quietly as I could, and walked over to the window that showed the monstrous cement parking lot with rows of ugly city lights beyond.

There was so much noise here. Rushing cars. Screaming ambulances. Humming electric everything.

Nothing and no one was going to keep me trapped here alone. If Adam left, it would be with me.

Before I'd become the world's most forgotten recluse, I'd been rather popular in my own way, and very much a City Girl. Some things stuck. I knew how to make people like me, even if I hated myself a little more every time I did.

On the bedside table between the bed and the desk where Adam had dropped my basket of belongings, there was an old, corded hotel phone. I unplugged it before anyone thought to call me.

Then I unplugged the TV too.

It was still too bright and noisy in a room that smelled of plastic and cheap cleaning agents.

I looped back to the window to check the parking lot.

Adam's car was there.

He wasn't.

The inevitable banging on the door came sooner than I'd anticipated. He must have taken the stairs. Good for him.

"Yes?" I said as I opened the door. "Have you changed your mind?"

Adam wasn't even breathing heavy, but his face was twisted into an irritated scowl, green eyes burning. "Give me my keys."

"I don't know why you're cross with me. You're the one who dropped them in my basket." I held the door open so he could go and retrieve them. "See? This is called being helpful and polite. Perhaps you'd like to reciprocate and give me a ride back home?"

"No." He walked out, slamming the door behind him.

The next bang came only sixty seconds later. He must have run the stairs this time.

"Yes?"

"Where's my key fob?" Adam held out the keychain missing the all-important drive component that worked as an anti-theft and anti-abandonment device.

"It fell off, remember?"

"And you picked it up. Now give it back."

"I really do not wish to be left here," I said evenly. "Perhaps this is a sign you should take me back with you. Don't you think it makes more sense to take me back? There's hotels and rentals closer to the mountains."

"Those are all filled with firefighters and the emergency crews." He pushed past me to go rummage in the basket for his key fob. "What is this?" He held up a book with foil-embossed flowers on a black cover.

"A book?"

"Magical Flowers," he read the title out loud in case I didn't recognize it. "Fiction?"

"Hardly. It might be classed as folklore under some broader definitions. Really, it's a reference manual. There was a take-one-leave-one bookshelf at the back of the community center where we stopped last."

He found the black key fob. "Thank you. Enjoy your book."

"A sensible person might wonder if I was a witch who was going to hex you."

"I'm sure you're a good witch."

"I will be, if you get me out of this city and somewhere quiet before I lose my mind."

He stopped a few feet from me, studied the ceiling, squinted as he struggled to think... Then shook his head. "Nope. That's still a no from me. Take a hot bath. Get some good. Sleep. In the morning you'll agree I made the right choice."

Somehow I managed to find the self-control to grind my teeth together. "I'll consider that. As soon as you agree to get me out of here."

"Not happening."

"Then allow me to wish you good luck with your drive home." My vicious smile as he walked out the door was completely wasted on the back of his head.

I didn't bother to walk to the window. Alone again, my knees were wobbly. Everything in this place was designed to stress me out.

Maybe a bath was a good idea after all. I ran one, using the hotel's soap assortment to make a truly luscious bubble bath. I found one of my old playlists on my phone, hooked it up to the ensuite speaker system, and blasted an orchestral arrangement with heavy percussion at a volume designed to block out all other noise without getting myself evicted by management.

With the lights off and my phone creating a star map on the ceiling, I could sink into the bath. Let the waters soak away some of the terror. Let the familiar sounds drive away the cacophony of the city and the banging on the door.

I dropped under the water.

Thump. Thump. Scream.

I popped up.

On the edge of hearing it almost sounded like someone was calling my name. How odd.

I slipped back under the water with a smirk, muscles finally unwinding ever so slightly.

Light cut through the darkness.

I surfaced and stared across the bubbles at Adam standing in the doorway to my bathroom with the door to the hotel room wide open behind him. "Did you change your mind?"

"Give me my starter." He tried to loom. It probably worked well on other people, he had the height for it, and I could see frustration in his eyes, but he was about as intimidating as dandelion fluff. His eyes kept dropping to the bubbles as his cheeks turned pinker under the scruff.

I splashed the water just enough to show a little leg.

He took a sudden interest in the ceiling. "I just need my starter."

"Your starter?" I tilted my head in confusion. "Is that an appetizer or are you hoping I'll write you a pick-up line?"

"The starter to my car." He made eye contact, nudity apparently forgotten.

"You already took your keys. Remember? I was begging you not to leave me here and you decided to rummage through all my worldly possessions?"

He stopped, took a deep breath, and stared at me incredulously. "Do you seriously not know what a starter is? In a car engine?"

"Do I like someone you'd believe knows about cars?"

"You seriously..." He bit off his argument with a shake of his head.

"Seriously."

His glare turned to a full scowl. "Fine!" He stomped into the room to dig through my clothes again.

"At least close the door!"

There was a hearty curse from the main room and then more stomping. The hotel room door slammed shut, but not the bathroom door.

Clearly I wasn't going to get any peace even if Adam stayed. With a heavy sigh, I stepped out of the bath and reached for my towel in an attempt at decency. "How did you even get in here?"

"I told the front desk my girlfriend fell asleep and I'd left my key in here."

"So, you're adding assault to your kidnapping repertoire?" Giving up on drying my hair, I wrapped the towel around myself and stepped into the main room to glare at him.

He did a fantastic job of only letting his eyes stray from my face twice. Truly a heroic effort considering the distraction in front of him.

"I rescued you."

"After I distinctly told you not to."

"Where is my car starter?"

"Maybe that's what I'm doing wrong," I said, ignoring him. "Maybe I should tell you to leave and then you'll force me to go back with you."

"I will leave as soon as I find the piece of my car you stole." He stalked towards me.

It was strange. I should have felt threatened, but he was about as intimidating as the average hummingbird. In theory he could do damage. I just didn't see that happening today.

"What," he demanded in a low growl, "did you do to my truck?"

"What makes you think I know anything about car engines?"

"Because I don't believe in gremlins. Someone got under my hood, took the starter, and walked away. I'm betting it's the lady who wants me to stay with her."

"What I want is for you to kindly drive off a cliff and die. I'm willing to settle for you undoing the damage and returning me to my home." I opened the hotel door for him. "You said we were friends, that was a lie. You said you'd take care of me, that was a lie. You said I needed to come with you for safety. I wonder if that was a lie too."

Adam opened his mouth to argue, then shook his head and stalked out of the room.

If nothing else, we were even. I didn't want to be here and neither did he, but at least we were stuck in this misery together. That was balance of a kind.

I slammed the door shut, engaged all the locks, and plugged the phone back in so I could call the front desk and tell them the angry man they'd allowed in was not, in fact, welcome here at all.

He'd thoroughly tossed the room looking for the spark plug, which only made a mess. When I went to brush my teeth before bed, I checked the water tank of the toilet. The starter bobbed cheerfully in a sealed plastic bag.

I'd said no one would believe I knew about cars.

I didn't say they'd be right.

Morning came far too early, heralded not by the quiet morning sun over the Calapooya Mountains but by the screaming of an ambulance siren at four in the morning. I'd tried going back to sleep but everything was wrong. The pillows were the wrong kind of fluffy. The bed sheets smelled of the wrong kind of soap. The noises in the darkness were the wrong kind of noises.

Enraged, I got up and made it everyone else's problem.

By the time I showered and dressed, I had something like a plan in mind. My parents' lawyers that I had inherited were on the east coast, so at least it was working hours.

Probably.

It was late December and I had a nagging feeling that the average American was doing something other than grading final essays this time of year. My entire life had revolved around school schedules, with holidays like Pi Day,[17] Golden Ratio Day,[18] and International Literacy Day,[19] or the classic Spring, Summer, Fall, and Winter Breaks. I was aware several religions had holidays in December but they'd never featured into my life after age six and the only holiday songs I knew were in Spanish.

I picked up the hotel phone, dialed the number, and waited.

---

[17] March fourteenth.
[18] July eighteenth.
[19] September eighth.

"You've reached the law offices of Bear, Rasp, and Jeong, how may I direct your call?" The receptionist had a high tenor voice that sounded a little hoarse. Maybe the nagging feeling was because I'd forgotten a sports holiday. When did football fans celebrate their rivalries? Was that December?

It didn't matter.

"This is Phoebe King. Connect me to Gwenda Rasp." Belatedly I remembered manners might help. "Please."

"Connecting you now."

The hold music stretched, playing some symphony that sounded vaguely like something I'd heard at a Julliard concert when I was twelve. Maybe that meant it was popular. Or easily playable by any knucklehead who could tell which end of an oboe to blow in.

I pinched the bridge of my nose and recognized I was angry.

Being angry and letting the anger hurt other people were two different things. I could do better. I *could* do better.

Adam's mixed expression of frustration and disgust flitted across my memory.

Ugh.

"Miss King?" a woman asked on the other end of the line.

"Yes," I snapped. Breathing and mantras were not enough to get me through this day. "Who is this?"

"Gwenda Rasp." My memory pulled up the image of a woman in her mid-forties with raspberry hair cut in in a curly pageboy crop that put me in mind of a mushroom. "For security purposes, would you mind giving me your account number?"

"Yes, but I'll give it to you anyway." I rattled it off from memory. "I had to evacuate the cabin because of a wildfire and I need to reintegrate into the populace. I suppose. The most pressing issue is ensuring my accounts are open for me, and then I need to do something about this TV show that is running with my IP.[20] I'm meeting with my literary agent in a few hours when she's awake. What can you do for me?"

Over in New York, Gwenda must have opened my files to see who she was dealing with. "Miss King, yes. You're a long-time patron of our firm."

"Third generation. My account was set up the week I was born." Because my parents did understand that generational wealth was to be guarded with a firm but fair hand.

"I'll have my team review everything and have a precis emailed to you before noon, eastern. Will your contact information remain the same?"

"My email is the same. My address is unfixed at the moment—"

"We have a partner firm in San Francisco," Gwenda said. "Would you like to use their offices as your physical address for the time being?"

"For now," I agreed. "I don't currently have a working phone, but I'll have that fixed in a few hours. My number should remain the same. If it changes, I'll let you know."

"Excellent. Is there anything else?"

"Not yet," I said. "But things may change rapidly. The TV show using my IP is making announcements this week and I need to make sure I've not lost the rights to my work."

"I fully understand, Miss King. Know that Bear, Rasp, and Jeong are here to support you throughout this. We will ensure you are protected throughout the process."

"Thank you."

"Do you have any property concerns?"

I hesitated for only a moment. In for a penny in for a pound, I supposed. "I'm not aware of what I still own

---

[20] Intellectual Property—if you didn't know, you own the things you create. I own the things I create. Now you know.

except for the cabin. There's fire insurance, but I signed a waiver for the local fire department. They aren't required to do anything to save the property. When the wildfire is contained, we'll want to send someone out to view the property. There's not much else to do beyond that."

"Mmm," she made an almost-agreeing sound. "I'll send you the list of your other properties along with the precis. You're currently in northern California?"

"A little north of Redding," I said.

"You don't own anything there."

"I didn't expect to." I brushed a hand over the trim, russet-brown slacks I was wearing. "I won't be here long. I just want to handle everything while I'm in town."

"Of course. Will that be all?"

"Yes, thank you. Have a good day."

Gwenda murmured her goodbyes and I hung up.

It was almost six thirty.

I went down to the breakfast bar to grab something to bring back upstairs and saw Adam. Double ugh.

He sat in the far corner overlooking the closed cement patio, eating some oatmeal that smelled of cinnamon and berries even from across the room.

Grabbing a bagel, cream cheese, and an orange, I crossed the room to his table.

Adam looked me up and down, the expression of mild surprise seemingly frozen on his face.

"May I sit?"

"It's a free country." He stuck his spoon in his oatmeal and sat back.

I raised an eyebrow in question as I smeared the schmear on my bagel. "Problems?"

"Nope. Just wondering when you're going to give me back the pieces to my truck. I slept in the truck bed last night. I'm looking forward to heading home and vanishing into the woods."

"At least it was your own bed," I said cheerfully before I took a bite. Was the feral smile with my teeth showing necessary? No. Did it make me feel better? Yes.

Wildfires burned in the forests of Adam's eyes.

I really needed to stop noticing those eyes. It was only going to lead to trouble.

"Can I have my starter back now?"

I weighed the options for a minute more. "Maybe."

"Maybe?" Adam's eyebrows went up in surprise and he leaned forward. "Maybe? Listen, Sunshine, you vandalized my truck after I saved your life. Most people would have reported you to the police."

"I told you to leave me up in the mountains in my cabin. Your choice to abduct me had consequences and they are entirely your own problem."

"And I am entirely willing to leave right now. Just give me the starter for my truck."

"You misunderstand the nature of your problem. You dragged me away from my home and back to the living hell of the rest of the world. I don't want to be here. You decided I needed to be though, so here I am. Your problem. We already agreed to that."

He grimaced but didn't disagree.

Picking apart my bagel, I steeled my nerves and presented my solution. "You propose to leave and make this misery my problem. I have a counter proposal: stay."

Adam snorted, starting to laugh until he saw my expression. Then his face fell into a look of polite horror. "Are you serious?"

"How much do you make in a year doing your tour guide thing in the forest?" I finished nibbling at my bagel as he weighed his options.

Credulity seemed to win and he answered, "Around two hundred thousand in a good year. Some of it goes to equipment and permits, but usually I take home a decent chunk of it. Why?"

"What would you think if I paid you fifty thousand a day to stay with me for the next three weeks?"

"I'd think you were insane."

I shrugged. "You should have realized that the first time you saw me. The warning signs were there. In multiple languages. Does anything I do seem rational to you? It shouldn't have. No matter." I waved my nervous oversharing aside. "The offer still stands."

"Why?"

"Because you hate me."

Adam's eyebrows threatened to crawl to the ceiling. "I'm sorry. I misheard you."

"You didn't."

"Right." He took a deep breath and blew it out like that would somehow fix the world. "Okay. Great. That makes no sense."

"It makes perfect sense. In a few hours, I'm going to walk into a very fictional life. One created by fans, and speculation, and people who needed to spin stories about who I am to sell things."

He squinted at me. "What?"

"You know *All These Broken Seasons*?"

"Yeah. Great series. I've read it a dozen times."

"I wrote it. With my dad."

His eyebrows were going to be sore from doing all these push-ups.

"My mother had brain tumors."

I don't know where that came from. I didn't mean to tell him the whole story, but the dining area was empty except for us.

The truth tumbled out. "She was in the hospital off and on for years. In the final few years, she lived there year-round. On her good days she could teach lectures. On her bad days she was aware of everything around her, but trapped in her body. Unable to move, speak, do anything.

But she could hear." I took a deep breath and tried not to feel all the old ghosts of my childhood crowding around me.

"My dad and I sat with her in shifts. He sat with her in the mornings, and lectured in the afternoons. I took classes in the morning, and did my homework by her hospital bed. We rotated sleeping with her or in the apartment down the street. She didn't see very well, especially on the bad days, but she could visualize things. So we took to reading to her. When we ran out of books she liked, we switched to telling her a story. My father wrote it down so I could keep track of scenes. We built a world where she was the queen."

"The missing queen from the first book?" Adam guessed.

The memories felt distant and cold, but I nodded.

"We told her the story of her illness in fantasy, hoping she'd recover. But," I took a deep breath to steady myself, "she didn't. She was alive when we started the second book. We meant to write about her recovery, but it never came. The queen never returned."

"I'm sorry." He sounded like he genuinely meant it.

"So was I." The pain was still there, an aching wound that never seemed to heal. "My father and I kept writing. The books were a way to keep my mother with us. He did the author work: the social media, ads, contracts, con appearances, panels, all of that. I was a teenager, and working on my degree."

"Your high school degree?"

"My second doctorate." I waved the distraction aside. "I thought it was fun, you know? A little secret window into another world. Books four and five were mine. He was too busy then, between teaching at the university and handling book signings. He loved the publicity, the fans, the commotion of it all. He loved being in the center of the world they created for him because it meant he didn't need to deal with the grief of being a widower with a child at home."

"Who took care of you?"

"Me," I said. "Obviously."

Something in his eyes changed as the line of his shoulders softened. He understood. "I'm sorry."

"Hold that thought, we're not to the sad part of this story yet."

"We're not?"

"Nope." I shook my head. "The sad part hit later. When he was driving to a book event and announcing the series wouldn't end with book five, but with book six. He was in the hospital for three weeks while I sat there alone. I planned his funeral by myself. Packed his office. And I went up to the cabin."

Grimacing didn't stop tears from blurring my vision.

"I went up there to pack my stuff and grab a few things before putting the cabin up for sale. Do you know what I found?"

"What?"

"Nothing." The pain of it hit me all over again.

The aching loss and the bitter, bitter resentment.

"I had walls of awards given to my parents. Photos of them throughout the years. Half of them were photos I took. The kitchen was filled with their favorite foods and recipes.

"But I wasn't there. None of my awards made it to the wall. None of my pictures were there with my mom and dad. I couldn't name a favorite food. I was taught not to have one. I was taught to eat what I had and be grateful because my parents took me along to their university dinners from the time I was born.

"I didn't have toys. I didn't have a favorite blanket. I didn't have anything I'd picked ever because my parents curated my life as well as any museum exhibit. I was a project they'd put together to show off at university events, carefully cultivated to make them look good.

"I was so angry. And you're not..." I almost bit off the words. "You're not supposed to be angry with your parents. I was supposed to be grieving these loving parents that had been the center of my whole world for twenty years, and I was angry with them. Angry for never letting me have anything of my own life. Angry that they died. Angry that I was alone with myself for the first time and I didn't know who I was.

"That's why I stayed. That's why I couldn't leave. I was scared of another car accident. And another hospital stay. But I was even more scared of trying to figure out who I was without being told who I was by other people.

"Then you, monster that you are, dragged me back here. Now I have to go back to it all. I have to step back into the life of Phoebe King, and I will have a million people telling me who they think I am. None of them know me. None of them care about me. None of them will understand. But you do." I looked at Adam. "You are the only person in the world who actually knows what I'm like. You know more about me than anyone, alive or dead. You will be honest with me. I need that right now."

Adam was already shaking his head.

"It's not that hard. You stick around, you drive the car for me, and you glare at people who try to get too close. If you have to flirt with me to make some guy back off, I'll double your day's pay."

"Driving you around? That's worth fifty thousand a day to you? That's a ridiculous sum of money."

"You said you'd like to vanish into the woods and never talk to another living soul again. Work for me for the next three weeks, and you'll have a million dollars in your pocket. Spend a month with me, and you can pay your taxes and keep a million in your bank account."

He leaned closer. "Can I get that in writing?"

"Absolutely."

Was it wrong to trust the random man who'd dragged me from my home with my safety as I waded into the world of celebrity and money? Probably. It was dangerous, certainly. Self-indulgent, definitely.

A better person probably would have done some yoga, centered their energy, and moved on. I wasn't a better person. I was a monster, and I was okay with that.

THERE WERE MEETINGS. VIDEO CONFERENCES. LEGAL BRIEFINGS. And money, lots of money, spent.

Monday rolled past, with Tuesday tumbling after; Wednesday washed over me, but Thursday rolled in with storm clouds on the horizon.

My to-do list was epic and I was losing the fight well before noon. By the time the six o'clock dinner rolled in, I was regretting not burning to death in smalltown Oregon.

"Walter Bay Hotel?" Adam peered through the windshield of the truck with a dubious expression. "I feel underdressed."

The Walter was one of the nouveau-riche hotels that had popped up in the economic boom of the late 2030's. Someone had bought a whole eastern-European castle and moved it to Winters, California, for the aesthetic. We were somewhere near Putah Creek State Wildlife Area with signs for the old Pleasure Cove Marina and Steel Canyon Resort. It was outside Sacramento and further south than I'd been in a decade.

Framed by towering redwoods and the distant purple mountains, the castle-turned-hotel looked like a Gothic cathedral had mixed genes with a Renaissance painting to create a turreted princess who could possibly hold off an actual army. Which was necessary, because there was an army of paparazzi at the front entry already.

Adam slanted a glance at me. "How do you want to do this?"

Event planning wasn't exactly within my skill set, but I'd attended formal events since I was three. As a rule the people throwing the elaborate celebration were not the people who did the cooking, cleaning, or decorating. "There." I pointed to a back lot with several vans labeled with Brontide Catering. "We'll go in through the service entrance."

"We can do that."

Since my unceremonious meeting-slash-abduction, we'd gone up in the world. We'd acquired two suitcases, a backpack that doubled as a laptop case, and an array of shoes that mostly lived scattered under my feet in the truck. Well, more like I'd acquired and Adam had rolled his eyes and reminded himself he was getting paid to be there. For fifty thousand a day, he was willing to be very tolerant of my moods.

I expected some trouble getting in. Or at least that one of the catering staff would try to shoo us away, but we breezed through the undercut of the castle. Check-in was done remote by the phone, and I typed in the door code to a two-bedroom suite with a shared living space and small kitchenette. A bay window looked out from the tower, with pine-green couches organized around a glass-top coffee table so someone could sit there and enjoy the view over the sycamore trees outside. Dark wooden doors opened right and left to rooms. One looked spring toned, with pastel greens and soft pinks; the other was darker, like the forests at midnight. "Right or left?"

"South for me." Adam nodded to the room on the left with the deep green shadows.[21] "When's the shindig start?"

"An hour," I said, mentally creating a to-do list for the next thirty minutes. "I'm going to get dressed and head down early. See if I can catch that showrunner who's in town. I know the studio execs are making most of the

---

[21] If I were writing this book, that's the room the assassin would pick. I tried not to overthink Adam wanting it. He probably just didn't want the buttercup-yellow pillows.

money decisions, but I think having the actual crew on my side would help. What was her name again?"

"Billie Boem." Green eyes met mine and I saw pity there.

My lips curled into a snarl.

With a sigh, Adam shook his head and closed his door. We'd had this argument multiple times.

My lawyers said that they could get the show killed, no problem. My literary agent and publishing house were happy to acquire the new books, generously. My problem remained with the studios that controlled *Shattered*.

Their marketing team was in love with the vote. The very problematic vote that showed that the world wanted the main character to die.

Everyone agreed the best option was to quietly edit the books in the background while the show ran its course and then release the books after the final season.

My agent called it 'Pulling A Georgie' and I called it 'Untenable.'

Working in my favor was the fact that the studio people all wanted to meet me. The first day had been hard, but when the author showed up looking "young and titty,"[22] everyone was eager to wine and dine me. So I let myself be wined and dined.

I hated it. I wanted to scream. I thought about gouging my ears out with the steak knife. I calculated how fast I'd need to run to achieve a fatal velocity going over the edge of restaurant's balcony. But I'd managed to smile through it all.

That's all that really mattered. People didn't care if I was screaming internally and hating every second of their

---

[22] I'm sure they meant pretty... No. I'm not. I knew exactly what they meant and I'd seriously contemplated asking Adam if he knew how to lose a body in the woods if I tossed in an extra cash bonus. I'd have killed them myself, but I didn't think I could lug a man twice my size to a car, let alone to an unmarked grave.

hand lingering on mine, as long as they were seen in public with a pretty young thing.

"No murder!" Adam called from across the living room.

I glared at the door. "How can you tell what I was thinking?"

"You're growling!"

With a sniff of dismissal, I snapped open my suitcase. My choices for the evening were a dark, pine-green pantsuit that verged on the edge of black, or a velvet, off-the-shoulder cranberry dress that made my bare skin glow and the red of my copper hair come out to play. There was a nice flow to the full skirt, with a high enough slit that I could show some leg if I needed to derail a conversation, and I liked the silky ruffles on my shoulders. A delicate gold necklace would have rounded it out nicely, but I didn't own any jewelry. Sultry eyes, dark lips, hair in a chignon, and done in fifteen minutes.

Stepping out into the main room of the suite, I saw Adam buttoning up a white shirt with his bedroom door open.

He glanced at me and his gaze caught.

I spun slowly. "What do you think?"

"It gets the job done." The words were casual but his voice was the right kind of rough. His gaze ate me up.

For a split second I imagined a world where we'd met in a different way. Imagined what would have happened if we'd talked in the hardware store months ago instead of meeting between fires and doom.[23] Imagined a life where he was looking at me and not simply tallying what my outfit cost.

With a sigh, I forced a smile. "See you downstairs."

"Sure thing, Sunshine." He turned away without another word.

---

[23] Not a complete exaggeration. The books were the only thing I had left and the only legacy I was likely to leave in the world. Losing them to someone else felt like burying myself all over again.

I went out, mentally arranging my invisible armor. Nothing said could hurt me. Fury was the mind killer. I would remain calm. I would smile. I would praise these people and win them to my cause because murder was still illegal, even if you were really, really angry.

And I was burning with rage.

On the ride down in the elevator I closed my eyes, swallowing down the bitter gall of it all. How dare they take the only thing that was mine? How dare they replace me? How dare they rewrite my life for their convenience? All of that got pushed deep, deep down with the memories of my quiet mountain house and the books I'd left unread. I buried all the pain and rage under a saccharine smile.

Show time.

The main ballroom of Walter Bay was part of the original castle, with a low ceiling of wood carved in a repeating geometric design. The floor was dark gray stone. The effect was rather like being buried alive, but I didn't think that's what they were going for.

I wove through the catering staff, trying to find a recognizable face. Billie favored bright looks from Avidan, the ones that had the black outlines so everything from her dress to her purse looked like a cartoon drawing. Her neon pink dress stood out in a sea of darker, wintery colors. Her makeup didn't quite match and I wasn't sure if I was disappointed or not. Either way, she was easy to find in a crowd.

"Billie?" My voice was soft, my smile warm. Practice made perfect after all, and I'd had lots of practice.

"Phoebe! Darling! Bright delight!" Billie raised a glass of pink wine and air kissed me from two feet away. "Love this color on you!"

"Thanks."

"Did you talk to my designer?"

"Of course." Long enough to know that I didn't want to wear a cartoon dress, at any rate.

"Do you want a drink? Wine? Beer? Limecello?"[24]

"I'll wait until dinner." Less drink in my hand meant less chance of me throwing a glass of something in someone's face.

Billie waved away a waiter.

"About *Shattered* and the vote," I said, skipping all the usual pleasantries. "I would love some insight on your writing team's plans. What's going on in the writing room?"

"Open warfare." Billie polished off her glass of wine and signaled for another. "Let me tell you, your sudden resurrection did not help. Everyone wants something. No one wants the same thing. Several of my best are shopping new scripts so they can escape."

"Are they not being paid well enough?" I could fix an income issue. There was money from the original deal set aside specifically for bonuses and to augment funds in case this happened.

Billie shook her head, black curls bouncing above her shoulders. "It was easier with the books to follow."

"So having the new books would, theoretically, fix the problem?"

"There's—oh!" Billie waved at someone behind me.

I turned to look at the growing crowd and when I turned back Billie had been replaced with a man in a duck-egg blue suit and pale yellow shirt. I was mildly disappointed he didn't follow through and wear rubber ducky shoes, but they were a butter yellow, so he got a C-minus for effort. He had dark brown hair slicked back with the sides shaved short and a cologne that was as repugnant as his smirk. "You said you were Phoebe? David's daughter?"

"I don't think we've been introduced." My smile stretched thin.

---

[24] If you know, you know.

"Jack." He grabbed my hand and shook it. "Jack Kasko. I'm the biggest fan of *All These Broken Seasons*. Hugest. I have an award even." He kept a death grip on my hand as he laughed.

"So pleased."

"Listen, I've been working with the show. And I'm excited you're back. Truly. Your dad and I go way back. I'm sure he mentioned me."

"I don't seem to recall that." I shook the man free of me and stepped back.

He stepped closer again. "We hung out. I gave him ideas for the fifth book. I didn't want to take credit, but we talked about the whole plot one night at a con."

"For the fifth book?" I couldn't keep the doubt from my voice. "My father didn't write much of book three or four. He had nothing to do with book five."

Jack laughed and grabbed my arm. "You're cute. I like that. Funny!"

"Please let go of me." Brushing him off with a frozen smile, I looked for an escape.

Everyone else was lingering about. Chatting. Drinking. Not helping.

Where was Adam?

I searched the room and caught sight of him standing along the wall, watching the whole charade in silence.

Sidestepping Jack's ramble about how he loved being the stand-in author advisor, I headed towards Adam and escape.

"Wait!" Jack matched strides with me. "Look, why aren't you listening?"

"Because you aren't who I'm here to speak with?" I blinked at the man in confusion. "What do you want? An autograph? A fan memento? A photo? I appreciate that you, along with several other million people, love the books and show. That has nothing to do with me or the business I'm here for."

He laughed loud enough to draw attention from bystanders. "Your business is my business!"

The manners mother had insisted on came to the fore. "I don't see how." My voice was melodic, charming, dangerously polite.

"You're making changes to my books!" Jack said. "To my show!"

"You're the showrunner? I thought Billie was in charge. Minerva Kline is the head of the legal team handling contracts for the studio. Baxter Krist the head of the finance team. There's two Daniel Martins on the ad team, and a Becca L'Hare is handling the Canadian ads. There's no Jack Kasko on the lists. I do have quite a good memory."

"I love those books more than anyone in the world!"

"I created those books," I countered in an even tone, my small smile ever-present. "I imagined the characters. I created the world. I scribbled down the notes. I told the story."

Jack moved closer, a sympathetic smile on his lips and rage in his eyes. "You don't understand. Girl math, right? Your daddy wrote the books so you think you understand them."

"My father and I wrote the books together."

"Sure. Cute. I get it." His arm went around my shoulder. "I'm sorry."

Punching him in the balls in the middle of a crowded room would probably land me in jail, so I ever-so-politely stepped out of his reach. "You're forgiven. Think nothing of it."

"I promise I'll forget. We're going to work together. I'm sure it's hard for you. But I'm going to take care of you."

"That isn't necessary." I turned and all but ran to Adam.

Green eyes met mine and Adam pushed away from the wall.

I stopped from slamming into him, barely, and went on tiptoe, hands balanced on my chest. "How much for you to pretend to be my boyfriend?"

"What?" His arm went around my waist as I teetered. His eyes were still over my shoulder.

"There's a man here who won't take *no* for an answer and I don't want to go to jail for murder. How much money to play my jealous boyfriend who doesn't share well?"

His eyes met mine and for just a moment I thought I saw something like hunger. He licked his lips.

If he kissed me... My breath caught in anticipation.

A sardonic smile replaced the hungry look. "For you, Sunshine, I'll keep it cheap." He'd said the same thing about the six-hundred-dollar pants I bought him on Monday.

"An extra twenty-five thousand a day?"

"Sure."

"I'll add an addendum to the contract when we get upstairs."

"Sounds good."

If my gaze caught on his lips, I only had myself to blame for the one-sided temptation. Curse my useless attraction to unavailable people.

"Phoebe!" Jack's whine knocked me back to reality.

"Do it for the show," I whispered to myself. Then I smiled, leaned in to kiss Adam's cheek and turned to face the world I wanted to set on fire.

FOR THE SHOW.

"There I am, in my pajamas, reading the last Natalie Zane book because I need to catch up before I read the new one." I held out a hand to the table of fake admirers as I ignored the over-priced, under-flavored dinner on the table. It was true that I was no actress, but I could fake it like an amateur on fight night when I needed that prize money. Or the approval of strangers who had a throttle hold on the future of my intellectual property.

"Don't we all," Billie interjected.

"She's such a good writer!" I could play Bookish Fangrrl[25] with the best of them. "We need to talk ships after dinner."

Billie nodded eagerly. "For sure!" Her eyes had the dull, terrified look of someone who had been taken hostage.

"Anyway, I'm there reading, and there's a banging at my door. And who shows up?" I waved a hand towards Adam and the entire table turned to him in surprise like he hadn't been sitting there for the past hour, or like he hadn't to fight Jack Kasko for the right to sit next to me.

My brain caught up to my current predicament. I'd told them Adam was my longtime, serious boyfriend, which meant I couldn't tell them the truth.

Adam's green eyes danced with delight as he realized I'd backed myself into a corner.

---

[25] Like a Fangirl, but more likely to break your arm to get that signed hardcover. Sometimes violence was the answer.

With a smile I reached for my water glass and silently toasted him. "Do you want to tell them?"

Laughing, Adam said, "She was oblivious. Her phone was dead. It's been dead since, when?"

"Oh, who knows." I shook my head. "It's been dead for years. Ever since I dropped it in the pond trying to take pictures of tadpoles."

"And she has no sense of time when reading," Adam continued. "The fact that the lights had turned on around the house and it was noon didn't even break her focus."

"It's a good book!" I took another sip.

"She was completely unprepared for a trip to town. So we hustled down with the clothes I grabbed from our laundry pile." The addition of *Our* was cute. "Every place we went to was full up. We wound up in Redding." Adam shook his head at the shame of it all.

Billie sighed happily at the romance of it all. "How did you two meet?"

Adam caught my eye and raised an eyebrow. "You want to tell that story, Sunshine?"

No.

No I did not. But I could lie. "We met at the hardware store in town. I was in there trying to find something to fix a window pane that had come loose. I bumped into him, literally, and when life hands you lemon chiffon pie, you do not say no. Although, with those green eyes, I suppose he's more of a lime tart." I winked at him playfully.

A cough covered Adam's blush as he looked everywhere but at me.

As our tablemates tittered and confessed their own first meet-ups with their current significant others, Adam leaned over. "I don't think I'm that sour."

"No," I whispered back, "you're bitter. Like dark chocolate."

"You shouldn't judge a snack without a taste first."

"Snack?" I leaned back and looked him up and down. "Babe, you're a whole banquet." I winked again for our audience.

The waitstaff moved in, clearing our dinner plates and putting down something beige and melty. It looked utterly unappealing.

"Sussex pudding!" Billie all but cooed. "I bet you love these!"

I couldn't help the raised eyebrows or blinking. "Pardon?"

"Sussex pudding?" Her smile stretched thin. "Isn't it—Isn't it your dad's favorite? The favorite food of P.H. Davide?"

"No. My dad was from Colorado. His favorite dessert was carrot cake with cream cheese frosting. Mine's hot chocolate crème brûlée. No one in my family is from Sussex. Why... Why would you expect us to like an English pudding?"

"It's in the book," Baxter said. "*Favorite Foods Of Your Favorite Authors.* Jack wrote it. You know Jack."

Cold settled around me. "Jack Kasko? Yes. We met today. For the first time."

Adam coughed, trying to break the tension. "What time is it, Sunshine? Mine's dead." He waved his blank-screened phone for all to see.

Pulling out my phone, I glanced at the clock. "After nine, why?"

"I promised my mom I'd call her and check in."

"Oh." His mom? He'd never mentioned parents to me.

"Do you mind if we go upstairs?" Adam asked the table. "We can come back."

"Oh! No! Don't worry about it!" Billie was already standing to shoo us away, relief written all over her face.

"I'm so sorry," I lied. "Dinner was lovely. I enjoyed getting to know all of you. But, Adam's mom is worried about the fires. She's up north."

"North of Portland," Adam added. "She's safe. She worries about us."

Someone snickered as Adam's arm wrapped around me.

"Enjoy dessert!" I waved goodbye and ignored all the murmurs about the dessert Adam was having.

His arm dropped the second the elevator doors closed. "Sorry about that."

"No worries." I handed him my phone. "Call your mom."

He pushed my hand away. "I don't have one."

"What?"

"Adam is a common name that starts with A. I was born at Sandlake Hospital, near a lake."

I blinked. "It's not a family name?"

"Yeah, no. I was less born-in-the-hospital and more dumped-in-their-Safe Baby-box when I was a few days old. I had foster homes, but I didn't ever have a family. There's no mom to call. I just wanted to get you out of the table before you used your dessert fork on everyone's favorite fan."

"Ah. Thank you." I took a deep breath and let my shoulders relax. "Aggressive men are meant to be dealt with using cold smiles and iced water. Using a knife is a felony. I assume a fork isn't better."

The elevator dinged softly and I stepped out in the cool—blessedly empty—hall. The night of fake smiles was officially over.

My social smile fell as the door to our suite unlocked. I was done. I needed to be done peopling for the next twelve hours, minimum. No one who could make demands of me. No one who needed me to behave.

"Why do you let them treat you like that?" Adam asked as the door locked behind me.

"Like what?"

"The whole greasy grabfest."

I took a water bottle from the fridge in the ensuite kitchenette and shook my head. "I don't understand the question. Jack's a guy. That's just how men are."

"It's not how I am."

"I know, which makes you amazing." I drank, trying to articulate what every little girl knew from childhood. "Look, I was seven the first time an old man pinched my bum."

"Bum?" He sounded incredulous that I didn't use a cruder term.

"It's the word my mom used." I shrugged off the implied rebuke with the gross feeling of the memory. "He was a professor emeritus at the university my parents were visiting, and he told me in another ten years I'd be just his type. I told my parents and my mom told me I was a good girl for not making a fuss. I was pretty, and the price of pretty is people seeing your body, not you."

Adam stared at me, eyes wide.

"It's just how it is. People accused me of flirting to pass classes I could have taught. I had someone file a complaint about an academic award because she thought I'd won it because of my tits. I was fourteen and it was for grad school.

"Men touch me all the time. It's why I let my dad go to the book readings without me. When I go out, they touch me. They bump into me. They molest me. No one ever asks. They assume it's the right they have to my body because I'm alive and pretty."

"I'm sorry. For earlier." Adam had stepped back, almost retreating to his room.

"For what earlier?"

"The arm around you, and"—he waved a hand—"the touches. I should have asked."

I rolled my eyes and slumped into the uncomfortable couch. "You're getting paid to be my boyfriend. I can handle the touching. With you at least I can be blunt and you won't care. You can't dislike me any more than you do." I held my water bottle up. "Every time I annoy you, remember this is your penance for saving me. You should have let me burn. Everyone would have been happier."

"That's not true." He said it softly enough I could pretend I hadn't heard.

But I didn't feel like playing pretend. "Tell me, in all the conversations this week, has anyone said they're glad I'm back on the scene? I know they talk to you. They flirt. You flirt back."

"I'm polite back, that's not the same as flirting."

Yeah, we were skipping right over the implications there. "What do they say about me? Anything good?"

Adam put his hands behind his back, leaning against the wall and avoiding eye contact.

"That bad?"

He shrugged, curling his lip at the thought. "It's, you know, whatever. They don't know you."

"No one knows me," I said.

"They think they know you," he argued. "So they get the wrong idea."

"They see a beautiful woman, assume she's stupid, and then get upset when I don't do what they tell me because they think I'm a pretty doll they can play with."

His gaze met mine and I knew he saw daggers there. "Yeah. People are stupid sometimes."

"And?" I could see he was biting something off.

With an eye roll he said, "And you're too nice. You're perfectly polite. You let them use you. You let them whisper about you behind your back."

"Fighting them won't change anything. I've tried it. It never works."

"Why not find better people to be around?"

"I did." I held my hand out to the empty room. "Everyone I trust is in this room. Everyone who has ever been kind to me is in this room. And, of the two of us, I'm not sure who hates me more. Probably you. But, right now, I'm regretting not jumping out of your truck before it hit the highway. This life sucks. I want a different one."

"So make a different one."

I opened my mouth to argue when someone pounded their fist on the door.

"Phoebe?" The voice had the familiar whine of Jack Kasko. "Phoebe, open up! I know that's not your real boyfriend! He's not your type!"

Adam and I shared a look of resigned frustration.

"I could punch him," Adam said quietly.

"You'd go to jail. You're not a very good bodyguard from jail."

"You could call security."

"There's paparazzi and cameras everywhere. Probably following him. They'll spin it to make him sympathetic. The sweet, lovable fan and the spoiled rich girl who ruined daddy's books." Never mind the reality of who wrote what.

Jack pounded on the door again. "Come on, Phoebe!"

I finished the last dregs of my water. "Unbutton your shirt."

Adam raised an eyebrow.

"Shirt unbuttoned, belt off, kick your shoes over there." I kicked my heels off.

"Nylons." Adam nodded to my legs. "Hair down."

"Hair down? Why?"

"Because it's the first thing I would do if we came upstairs as a couple. I've been wanting to see your hair down all night."

I blinked as my cheeks burned. "Really?"

He nodded as he unbuttoned his shirt.

"Phoebe! *Phoeeee-beeee!*"

Adam reached out, then stopped. "Can I touch you?"

"Yes. I'll let you know when you cross a line."

He tousled my hair. "Perfect."

With a wink he stepped away, heading for the door. He jerked it open as Jack banged and yelled, and fell into the room.

"What are you doing here?" Adam demanded, his voice low and menacing. I knew it was all for show, but that didn't mean I couldn't enjoy it.

"What are you doing?" Jack used the wall to balance himself. He looked between me, perched on the back of the couch with my hair down and skirt dangerously high on my thigh, and Adam with his shirt open.

"What's it look like we're doing?" Adam asked. "Did you fail sex ed? This is the bit where we make out and have fun before we get sweaty."

"You're not invited to watch." I waved goodbye to Jack before he got any more ideas.

But apparently we'd used too many complex words for his alcohol-pickled brain, because the drunken fool pushed past Adam to glare at me. "Why are you doing this?"

"Why am I having sex with my boyfriend?" I tilted my head in confusion. "Because it's fun? Because I like him? Because I want to? Do I need a reason beyond, 'We're Both Consenting Adults Who Want This'?"

"What about me?" Jack demanded.

"I met you three hours ago," I said. "You're a random guy. Literally a random guy off the street. You read the book I wrote. You like the TV series. So do several million other people. Adam quite literally saved my life. He's my significant other and the only person I want touching me. He's also the person I was kissing when you started banging on the door."

"You're drunk," Adam translated for Jack as he grabbed him by the shoulder. "Go back to your room. Sober up. We'll pretend this didn't happen."

Jack pushed him away. "Phoebe belongs to me!"

"Phoebe woke up next to me this morning," Adam said.[26] "She's going to wake up next to me tomorrow.[27] The whole time, she's only belonged to herself. Nobody owns anybody. That's not how relationships work."

"But..." Jack looked honestly bewildered. "I had plans."

"Plan them with someone else next time," Adam advised. He turned Jack by his shoulders and led him to the door. "Goodnight."

The door slammed shut.

Adam locked it. He turned to look at me. "You okay?"

I nodded. "Thanks."

"Anytime."

My frazzled brain tried to pull something witty to say, but my eyes snagged on a bit of color peeking between Adam's pants and the dark hair on his chest. "Is that Bigfoot?"

"Hmm?" He froze in the act of running a hand through his hair, just out of reach. Glancing down, his grin turned wicked. "Yeah. That's Bigfoot with a bi-pride flag. For anyone who wants to go cryptid hunting in my forest."

"Uh huh." Why were my lips so dry suddenly? "Is that the only one?"

"No. I've got five. I'll get another one for my birthday in October."

"Mmm."

"Want a closer look?"

"Yes."

Adam stepped closer.

Reality slammed into me like a freight truck.

"Nope!" I slid off the back of the couch, stumbling backwards. "Nope! That would be wrong." I scrambled for

---

[26] True, but only because I fell asleep on the drive to where we stayed last night and we got there after one in the morning.
[27] I wished.

the safety of my room. "I should not sleep with an employee or anyone who hates me. This is a bad plan."

"Who hates you?" Adam asked as my shoulders hit my doorframe.

"You!" Reality sucked. I wanted to rewind sixty seconds and bite my tongue. "If you didn't hate me I'd climb you like a tree. I mean, you're what? Six two? Six three?"

"Six four."

"And look like you break rocks with your bare hands. You're rugged. You're my type. But you're employed by me. And you hate me. So we are not"—I waved a hand between us—"we are not doing this."

Adam nodded and stepped into his room, buttoning up his shirt. "Yup. Understood. Don't even worry about it."

"Right. Good." I nodded. "Sleep well."

"...Phoebe?"

"Hmm?"

"I don't hate you."

THERE WERE ONLY SO MANY WAYS TO RESPOND TO SOMEONE telling you that they didn't hate you when you told them that was the main reason you weren't sitting in their lap. I went with the very cowardly option of hiding in my room for breakfast, pretending Adam didn't exist.

It didn't help.

Apparently there was a ChristmasCon in Sacramento this weekend and Billie "would love" to have me on the stage. Someone named Kim Jihun[28] was "rattling the stars", according to the internet, with "shocking" pictures from Las Vegas.

I looked. The pictures were only shocking if you thought two hot men with excellent eyeliner kissing was shocking.

To be fair, the general internet agreement was that this was only shocking because Kim Jihun was supposed to be dating Iris Muhly. I was eighteen minutes into a video by someone called EveriReader detailing behind-the-scenes evidence and screenshots supporting the only ending that fit my books when another email popped up demanding my attention.

Reading through emails and fielding phone calls from Billie's team didn't improve my mood. Neither did dod-

---

[28] A famous Korean actor I had to look up after seventeen billion people asked me about him. He's cute, in a puppy-dog way. But he plays Valiant Verrat in the TV adaptation of my book series, so I guess I was supposed to know him as a person. I didn't.

ging repeated calls from Jack Kasko, who definitely should not have had my number.

There was a thumping from the main room.

A few minutes of thumping later, I heard Adam's growl and a surprised squeak.

"Jack is here," Adam said outside my door.

"Tell him I'm still in bed."

There was a brief argument on the edge of hearing. The door slammed shut.

So, hiding wasn't going to work. Time to put on my big girl panties and act like an actual adult. Ugh!

Adam was sitting by the kitchenette with a small glass of something that smelled berry-ish.

I nodded to him, dug around in the little fridge, and found nothing that looked edible.

"So..." I closed the fridge slowly as I tried to put together coherent thoughts. "About last night." I turned at looked at Adam.

He sipped his drink, expressionless. "What about it?"

"I think I may have gotten a little out of line." I'd sailed over our boundaries with a smile is what I'd done. It was atrocious and I knew it. "I apologize."

He nodded. "Okay. You're forgiven?"

"Just like that?"

"Just like that. I'm not worth worrying about." A cold smile flashed briefly across his face and he finished his drink. "You need anything from me today?"

"No—"

"Cool." He got up to leave.

"Wait!"

His glare probably made other people back down. Normal, sensible people, at any rate.

No one had ever accused me of being normal. "I didn't leave the room like that last night because I don't appreciate you."

"Lovely to look at but you want a no-touch policy? Fine. No worries." His face was blank, his voice flat as he washed out his cup and headed for his room.

Yesterday at least we'd been almost friends. He'd tolerated me. Now... Coldness settled in my stomach.

"Adam?"

"Hmm?" He stopped in the doorway, glancing back at me.

"I'll—" I took a deep breath. He didn't want to be here. He deserved to be free. I deserved to be free. The pain was spilling out of me. I was directing it at him, but that wasn't fair. I knew it wasn't fair. "I..."

He folded his arms as he turned to study me. Giving me the same look so many terrible men did when I turned them down.

I gave up. "You should have left me. I didn't want to be here. I didn't want all these enemies or any of this nonsense. But I'm here because of you. So I'm going to remain your problem. I'll transfer this next week's pay in bulk."

"Whatever you want," he said, voice unruffled. "You're the boss."

I nodded.

I was the boss.

I could do this alone.

We hit Sacramento early Saturday morning. Billie tried to get me to drive with her, but I'd insisted on staying with Adam, even though any onlooker would know there was trouble in Paradise.

It was a silent drive.

I was doing the right thing. Boundaries were important. I had money, social power, and a written contract making him my employee. The right thing to do was to not touch him. I wasn't supposed to use him for emotional support or have any desire to go caress his cryptid tattoos.

But, if I ended the contract, he'd leave. Like everyone else in my entire life, he'd take what he wanted, then vanish.

I'd be left mourning another death of what could have been. I couldn't handle that. Not today. Not while I was sorting through a thousand pages of legalese that boiled down to: yes, it's your intellectual property, but the studio will burn it to the ground if you ruin the vote.

The only way to get what I wanted was to sway the fans to my position.

So I went to Sacramento. I let the design team dress me up. I met with fans. Took pictures. Smiled on panels.

Ambulances screamed past. Watches ticked. Cameras clicked.

By Sunday afternoon I was ready to dive headfirst off the nearest ledge to escape. The only thing keeping me upright was Adam standing silently behind me.

"You okay?" he asked as we left another panel where I got to talk about my dead father for an hour to rapt fans who thought he'd hung the moon.

"Yes."

"The way you lie with a straight face worries me."

I rounded on him. "You don't—"

"Get paid to worry about you?" Green eyes were still cold as a winter forest, but at least they were familiar. "I do, actually. Quite well."

"That at least shows some foresight on my part." I turned to look down the long hall. It had bathrooms blocked off for the use of staff, important guests, and vendors, but it didn't have a stairwell that would get us away from the main con crowd. My phone pinged. I looked at it with rage and disgust.

"I'd tell you not to break it, but you can replace it," Adam said with mild amusement.

He deserved the glare he got. "I'd have to go stand in a store to replace it though, and that's probably worse. Why did you drag me away from my cabin?"

"Wildfire and a ninety-eight percent chance of death." The same answer he'd given me this morning and six times yesterday. But who was counting.

I opened the video my lawyer had emailed me.

Jack Kasko stared back with the con's banners in the background. He was running a fan panel for *Shattered*. Going on about how he knew the story better. He dismissed me. Made fun of me. Ridiculed me.

The phone manufacturer deserved a letter of commendation for building something that didn't spontaneously combust with that filth on it.

"This seems like certain death too." I handed the phone to Adam so he could see it. "My lawyer recommends making peace with Jack."

"What do you want to do?"

"Murder him." I sighed. "But I don't want to do jail time."

"Murder is bad for the soul."

"So is living with this much anger."

"Wanna yell at me?"

I shook my head. "You're the only person on the planet who tolerates me. I want to keep you."

"You'll forget about me soon enough."

Maybe he wanted to be the focus of my ire. Maybe the goal was to make me forget about Jack Kasko for a minute. Maybe Adam thought I looked hot when I was angry. Who knew?

He smiled when I glared at him.

"I can remember a book, word for word, after reading it once. I can recite the unabridged dictionary. I can name every single person I've met this weekend in the order I met them. Then tell you what they were wearing, what personal thing they told me, and how bad my signature looked on their swag. Forgetting would be a gift. It'd be a mercy if I could forget things people said to me. Things they did. But I can't. Maybe through concussive brain trauma I could fix that problem, but for now all I have is memories that eat me alive. So, please, tell me how on earth I'm going to forget the only person alive who seems to almost tolerate my presence."

A smart man would have bowed out of this fight.

Adam stepped forward, ready to do his three rounds in the ring. "Forgive me for not thinking your memory is that prodigious when I keep telling you that I don't hate you."

"Not hating is a long way from liking. And you're an employee."

"So burn the paperwork and pin me to a wall already. I'm fully onboard with you climbing me like a tree any time you're feeling athletic enough, short stuff."

"Short stuff?" I stepped closer, which didn't help my argument at all. "What happened to Sunshine?"

"I realized I could pick you up and fit you in my pocket, is what happened." Adam leaned over me.

"I hate how good you look."

"No you don't."

Light flashed down the hall. "Are you Phoebe King? You're Phoebe King. Hey!" the person shouted. "She's here! The lady that wants to ruin *Shattered*!"

Fortunately my education gave me the ability to swear in multiple languages. A boon at difficult times like these.

There was a crowd forming near the only exit.

"Want to leave?" Adam asked.

"Obviously."

He held out his hand.

I took it. He walked me towards the crowd as I braced for the inevitable litany of hate. People shouted, but they were still looking past me. Through me.[29] Somehow Adam had managed to have the one superpower I'd wanted since I was seven.

We walked through the crowd and down the main stairs without a single glance from the passersby.

"Told you I was good at being ignored," Adam said as we walked out to the street. "Where do you wanna go?"

"Anywhere but here, please."

"Sure thing, Sunshine."

Tears stung my eyes. For the first time in weeks, I felt safe, even with an ambulance going by.

---

[29] Was it weird? Yes. Did I hate it? No. Not at all.

Dry scrubland flew past us as we drove north on I-5 over the Sacramento River as silence filled the cab of the truck.

"So…" I was trying to process everything and words were not working.

"So?" Adam stayed on five, ignoring the exits for Woodland.

"You're a superhero?" I guessed.

He started laughing, face turning bright red. "What?"

"You turned us invisible to get us past the angry mob. That's a superpower, right?" It sounded like a superpower to me.

"Not the way I usually use it."

Intriguing. "What have you used it for?" I turned in my seat to study him.

"Uh, let's see: skipping class, theft, avoiding my ex in middle school, getting dumped because the guy I loved couldn't see me, literally. Losing just about every partner I've had because they forget I exist hours after they tell me they love me. Losing every job that requires me to show up daily because people forget I'm there. I've been told I'd be great at hide-n-seek if I ever played it."

"Can't you control it?"

"A little." He dodged around a truck driving slower than my dead grandma going down a mountain road in Mexico. "It takes more work to be noticed."

"Um… How do I put this politely… Have you seen a mirror before?"

"Yes."

"And people ignore you?"

"Yes."

"Weird."

He waved to my phone. "Look on social media. Check Everi1. Look for pictures of us. I've been with you at this con in public all weekend. There won't be pictures of me though."

"Impossible." Probably.

I opened the app anyway and scrolled through. Plenty of pictures of me. Most of them unflattering or loaded with lewd comments. But Adam was conspicuously absent. "Did they edit you out?"

"Nah, I just kind of vanish."

"So you are kind of a superhero?"

"I'm not a super-anything." He glanced at me and looked away quickly. "I really didn't think you'd notice. Or remember me. I thought you'd forget me that first morning. But you sat down for breakfast and hired me. If you stop paying me, you'll probably forget."

"I really don't think I will."

"Want to bet on it?"

Not paying Adam meant he wasn't my employee. It meant he could leave. It also meant there was no reason not to explore the look in his eyes. That sounded like an express train to a broken heart. But also weirdly tempting.

I chewed on the idea, unsure of the best option. Rather than answer, I found another topic to keep us busy. "Where are we headed?"

"There's a bed and breakfast I know up near the border. I rented it out for us for the rest of the week. I figured you'd need the break, and the fires are mostly under control. Once everything's done, you could go home."

An hour ago that would have been the best news in the world. Now it was... something else.

Turning my phone on silent, I curled up in my seat, pulling Adam's oversized jacket over me like a blanket. The way I had for a week now.

That was another thing to think about.

Adam had seen me at my worst. He'd seen all the ugly sides of me. He knew what kind of monster I could be. And yet he still went out of his way to help me. Kindly.

Sure, there was money involved, but now he was offering to get rid of that.

Which meant he either wanted to stay with me despite knowing what a terrible person I was, or he genuinely thought I'd forget he existed.

No, I supposed there was a third option: maybe he was going to have me cut the contract and would then leave, knowing full well I'd feel the sting of his abandonment.

"You're overthinking," Adam said.

"I'm thinking," I countered. "There's a difference."

"What's the worst that could happen?"

"You could abandon me, leaving me alone like everyone else I ever trusted, thus confirming every fear I've had for the past eight years."

"What's the best that could happen?"

I frowned at him. "Why does that matter?"

"If you're going to consider the worst case scenario, you also have to consider the best case. They're equally likely to happen."

"My life has consistently proven that people leave me."

"Doesn't matter. Worst Case or Best Case is like a coin flip. Previous coin flips do not influence the one you're doing now."

I stared at him from across the truck cab.

"What? I sat in on a stats class once! It's legit!"

"We should call you Sunshine, optimist." I rolled my eyes and curled back up under his jacket.

"Nah, I like ironic nicknames. You're a little ball of sunshine and death stares."

Pulling the jacket all the way over my head gave me a way to escape. I didn't want to think about Best Case Scenarios. I really didn't know what it would be.

It should have been going back to my cabin. Honestly, that was the best choice for me. I was safe there. No one could hurt me. No one could be hurt by me. It was exactly what I wanted nine days ago.

Now... Now I wasn't so sure.

There was a treacherous, wicked part of my heart that was whispering that a Best Case Scenario meant keeping Adam with me. But, unless that was his Best Case Scenario too, I couldn't have that. I was never going to hurt someone the way others hurt me. If I let someone love me, I might leave them one day, and then they'd be left feeling as alone as I had been for the past eight years.

It was better to stay unloved.

I WOKE FROM STRANGE DREAMS OF WANDERING SILENT FORESTS to see a Pacific Northwest winter scene, complete with an overindulgent powder-blue Victorian home spilling out into a mossy, flagstone driveway, surrounded by towering redwoods and ancient ferns. "Where are we?"

"Fort Dick."

"Excuse me?"

Adam grinned like a twelve-year-old. "That's the nearest town."

"There's a town named Fort Dick?"

"Yup." He hopped out of his car. "We're off one-ninety-nine between good ol' Jedidiah Smith State Redwood Park and the Tolowa Dunes."

My mental map of northern California was hazy, but dunes suggested ocean and I-5 was inland by a lot. "How long a drive is that?"

"About seven hours if you do the speed limit." Adam shut his door and stretched.

It wasn't full dark yet, and as the sun set around five this time of year, it was safe to say Adam hadn't followed the speed limits with exactitude. I tried to find a way to make that feel like a relevant concern, but the best I could summon was a shrug. We were here, wherever here was, and we were safe.

For a given value of safe.

All around us giant, ancient trees loomed as guardians. Sentinels of the forest. Silent wardens of a world not made by human hands. It made the turreted house with knee-high picket fence and pastel Christmas lights look far too much like a fairytale trap.

I mean, if I were a vengeful fey from an otherworldly realm bent on the destruction of humans, this is *exactly* how I would have decorated the house. Pastel lights, eco-friendly tinsel on a pine tree by the driveway, seashells and brown spiral shark eggs cases for decorations. Oh, no, those looked like seed spirals and millet, not shark eggs cases.

But this was definitely the kind of house that would decorate with egg cases and skulls.

The soft blue with vibrant white trim against the darkening sky did nothing to remove the aura of unspeakable danger. Or delight. It could go either way at this point.

Adam opened my door. "It's safe to get out."

"Sure it is. What's the name of this place?"

"Alfurheim Bed and Breakfast. Built by artist Eiður Alfurheim at the turn of the century." Adam was still grinning ear to ear.

"So, we're at Elf-Home Bed and Breakfast built by a man whose name means Oath Of The Elf-Home? In midwinter? In an ancient forest? Hmmm." I could spot a plotline from five hundred pages away and if this wasn't the opening to a new series, I didn't know what was. "Let's try to avoid any blood oaths or mead while we're here. My life is adventurous enough without inviting the elder gods in for dinner."

Adam burst out laughing. "It's a b-and-b decorated for Christmas. Not everything is a plot, Sunshine. This is just a holiday getaway."

"Uh huh. Yeah. I believe you. I've definitely never seen this movie."

He stepped closer, green eyes dancing with mischief in the falling light. "Should we find some mistletoe?"

"Hello!!!" someone sang out as the porch steps creaked. A woman with short blonde curls and a warm smile bounced towards us. Her bright green sweater with orcas wearing winter hats and Nordic sweaters was adorable. "I'm Connie Boronda! You must be the Sandlakes!"

"I'm Adam Sandlake." Adam held out his hand to shake hers. "This is Phoebe King."

"Girlfriend?" Connie guessed, reaching for my hand. "Fiancée?"

"Originally I was an abductee but he's growing on me," I said, shaking her hand.

Connie's eyebrows wrinkled in confusion. "Um…" She frowned at Adam.

"In his defense," I said before she attacked him, "there were extenuating circumstances like a wildfire threatening my home that I was trying to ignore. I've come to terms with the fact that he probably saved my life."

"Which is my problem," Adam said. "I saved her last week, so I also got the chance to save her from trouble at work today, and I'm convinced some time away from the city would be great for her."

"That's the perfect recipe for every holiday romcom, isn't it?" Connie's smile was infectious.

"I normally like cities," I said. "I'm just out of practice when it comes to being social."

"Well, you won't need to worry about that. You two have the whole house to yourself for the week. If you need anything, holler, I'm just down the way over there in the cabin by the crik."

"You hear that?" Adam asked. "There's a crik in Fort Dick!"

Connie laughed like it was the funniest thing she'd ever heard.

I shook my head and went to get my luggage from the bed of the truck.

Adam got to it first. "Upstairs or downstairs bedroom? There's only two."

"Upstairs is fine," I said. "But I might wake up in the middle of the night to raid the kitchen."

"You can wake me up in the middle of the night for anything. I'm not your employee this week. I'm just a guy in the same bed and breakfast as you." His smile was an invitation to pin him against a wall.

I narrowed my eyes as I considered it, but let him go.

Connie waved as she walked off with a final parting shot of, "Call if you need anything! It's no trouble!"

She was wrong. It was all trouble.

For the first time in years I was feeling that insidious, evil thing called Hope. I could picture a future, and I was disgusted with myself. Wanting things, hoping for things, believing in happily ever after was criminally stupid. I knew better.

But then I looked at Adam smiling as he held the door open and I forgot everything else.

Hopefully this really was a fairy home; I needed to be trapped here for a thousand years just so I could sort out my thoughts.

"What's that stormy look for?" Adam asked as I stepped into a house straight out of every horror movie.

Everything was so crisp, clean, and bright that it practically begged for the walls to start oozing blood. Seriously, no one really had lace curtains in their living room and butterflies on their summer-themed Christmas tree unless they were hiding evil ghosts in the attic.

"I didn't really grow up doing holidays."

"What did your family do?"

"Final exams and winter break. Which usually meant my parents were catching up on their own research or we attended winter galas. What about you?"

Adam shrugged. "Foster system kid. You know. Some local church would give us presents. I wound up with a haunted doll once. You know the old porcelain ones dressed like it's the eighteenth century? One of those, and a book on cooking for college for guys. I think the title was something like *Real Men Do Meat*."

"And that was a cookbook?" I didn't try to hide my surprise. "Sounds like erotica."

"It had hotdog recipes."

"Not helping, babe."

"Babe? Did I just get babe'd?"

"Don't read into it."

His chuckle was only mildly sinister considering the circumstances. "I'm growing on you."

"Like a fungus." Fear twirled across the stage of my mind like the Sugar Plum Fairy. "Doesn't that worry you? You think I'm going to forget you at any moment. Shouldn't you be avoiding me?"

"I tried, remember?" Adam took my luggage up the narrow staircase and left it on the landing overlooking the entryway. "You stole my keys. Then you stole the starter to my truck. Then you paid me to stay. If you're going to put that much work into keeping me around, I'm going to stay. Why wouldn't I?"

"Because I'm a feral monster of a human being who has all the social graces of an enraged ogre and the personality of an incensed scorpion? There's nothing likeable about me. People don't stay around me. You deserve better." He really did. "And, as soon as you return me to my house, you can have better."

He walked down the steps rolling his eyes. "You talk so tough, Sunshine. But you've got nothing to back it up."

I glared at him.

He bopped my nose. "You're cute."

"I'm quietly plotting to destroy a man's career."

"That Jack guy?" Adam asked as he moved his luggage down the hall by the stairs.

I followed him, passing the front parlor, a formal dining room, and a very inviting kitchen that smelled of cookies. "Yes. He thinks he owns my books because he loves them. He wants the TV show to fit his vision. I did all the work, and he's being praised as the hero of *Shattered*. The one true fan who fully understands the author's vision."

"While not recognizing you're the author?" Adam's room was tucked in the back of the house, a little green hideaway with a pinewood bedframe with a king-sized mattress, a TV artfully hidden behind a photograph of the redwoods, and a window that overlooked the back garden of the house in all its wintery dry glory.

"Yes." I sat on the bed as Adam started to unpack. "It was fine when my father was alive. He handled all the publicity. I…" The words failed me. "I didn't like it."

"How much of what you didn't like was being ogled by old men because you were young and pretty?"

"Most of it."

He hung up a couple of plaid shirts in silence, thinking. "You don't have to answer this if you don't want to."

"Obviously."

"How much do you think your worldview is influenced by the fact that you never really had a chance to form an identity outside of the one your parents assigned you?"

I blinked at him. "How many college classes did you sit in on?"

"A bunch. It was free and I was bored. Answer the question anyway."

"I don't know. I never thought about it. I was always with them until my dad died. I didn't go to regular schools. We moved too frequently, and when they realized I was intelligent enough to master academic skills quickly, they decided I didn't need formal schooling. I had more freedom when I took university classes, but I was young, and I still lived with them."

"So your dad died and that was the first time you did anything as an independent adult? But you were treated like a mini-adult your whole life?"

I kicked off my shoes and moved to sit in the center of the bed. "I didn't say it was the ideal upbringing for a child."

"So what'd you do about that?"

"About what?"

"You knew it was wrong. You knew you were alone. You knew you had issues. What did you do about it?" Adam turned to look at me and he looked serious.

"I went to the cabin."

"That's it?"

I shrugged helplessly. "I guess... I didn't know what else to do." The thought bothered me. "I was taught how to do math and languages. I learned finance skills and basic cooking. I know how to politely address someone in twenty-four languages, but no one ever taught me about taking care of myself." I frowned. "Everything I did was for other people. How to perform for them. How to impress them."

"So you built an entire life and identity on being someone you weren't?" He kicked his luggage into the closet. "Meanwhile, I had the opposite. Everyone ignored me. No one cared what I did. I wasn't important enough that anyone remembered me. Everything I did was for me. I don't always make the best choices, but I figured if I was all I had, I should try."

"Where are you going with this?"

"I'm just saying, I don't really get your life. I've followed you around for a week and it's been the weirdest week of my life. That's saying something, considering I've spent my whole life in Oregon. I've seen some really weird nonsense. So you being weirder than that is impressive."

"Thanks? I think?"

He shrugged. "We've got a week here. The house has great reception. There's a list of local therapists you can call on the fridge. Why not plan on giving yourself time to make choices? It's your life. You don't have to live it the way other people told you to, but you do need to live it." His smile turned wicked. "Now, are you going to stay in my bed all night or are you going upstairs?"

"I'm going!" I scrambled off the bed, despite the temptation to stay. There were too many competing thoughts in my head right now for me to make good decisions.

"I'm going to make some tacos for dinner. You want some?" Adam called after me as I fled up the stairs.

I stopped on the landing, and looked over the balcony. "Do you make good tacos?"

"Yes!"

"Then yes!"

Life was hard sometimes, but choosing tacos was easy.

The upstairs room was grand, high-ceilinged with woodland greens and golden teak, fit for an empress and empty as the promise of any empire. It was too large, too cold, too empty to ever offer comfort. Every breath echoed as if I were the last living creature in the universe.

Ugh.

A day in the mountain retreat should have made me feel better. I liked isolation. I liked being alone. I liked it so much I'd convinced Adam to go for a hike.

But now that I was alone I was left with the emotions from my first-ever therapy session whirling around me like an unseen storm.

It was gross. All these years I'd so neatly compartmentalized things. Tucked anger away in a box. Folded up my feelings and stowed them in the overhead compartment like a good passenger on the airplane of life. Allowed the rage to simmer only long enough to heat my cheeks but never long enough to burn down the prison I was trapped in.

Now it was all spilled out across the floor of my mental space, looking ugly.

Really, the reason I'd pushed Adam out the door was because I was afraid I'd take it out on him if he stayed. Anger was a beautiful fire that burned away so many other unwanted emotions.

Anger was safe. But anger didn't build.

If I wanted a future—and annoyingly enough, it was starting to look like I did, despite my own absolute disgust at myself for that—then I needed to sort out this mess in my head so I could figure out how to build the future I wanted. Not the future my parents planned or the future the world expected of me, but the future Phoebe wanted.

Which was really hard to put into words. In the before-times I was careful about not wanting anything. Wanting led to disappointment when it couldn't be calendared in, or didn't fit the family aesthetic, or wasn't "really needed" according to my parents. They'd controlled everything from the foods I was allowed to have as favorites, to how I dressed, to how I was allowed to speak.

While I'd lived alone in the mountains I hadn't wanted much because of apathy fueled by depression.

Wanting meant hoping for something.

Hoping meant I might get hurt again.

I didn't want to get hurt. But, like a bone that healed wrong and needed to be reset, I needed to handle the pain so I could move on with my life.

Growling, I tried not to think about how much easier life would have been if I'd just gone to the stupid book signing with my father. Then I'd be dead with my parents. I would have been mourned by people who knew the public construct my parents made. Everyone would have had what they wanted.

Except...

Memories of Adam's smile over the past week presented themselves for consideration.

There was probably something wrong with tying my will to live to someone else's approval. That sounded sus. But, at the same time, thin threads of hope wove a... something of something. The quote escaped me.[30]

---

[30] I never bothered to look it up. It was some pseudo-intellectual nonsense anyway, so make up something you like. If it gains traction you can give me full credit. See? I was too trained as an academic!

Anyway, it wasn't my will to live that was in question. It was my will to live near other people and have an active role in my own life rather than just trying to remember to breathe until I died of natural causes.

If I wanted a better life, I needed to clean up this mess, and I did it all with the risk of failure, disappointment, pain, and shame looming like the four horsemen of the mental apocalypse. Death, Famine, War, and Pestilence sounded easier to beat.[31]

I shook my head.

"No time for this. I need to—" ...Do something. Make a decision. Talk to Adam. Choose a better life.

Was that what I wanted?

I looked up at the stars painted on the ceiling. "Okay, universe, I need a sign. I want one. Are we doing this or not? Am I heading for the hills or am I going back to my life?"

The city. The sounds. The people... The thought of it didn't make me want to scream quite as much anymore.

Someone banged on the door downstairs.

I frowned as I heard the front door open without the familiar sound of Adam hollering.

Footsteps echoed in the rooms below, then made their way to the stairs.

Light, quick steps not made by Adam. If it was Jack Kasko again, I was going to go look up local gun laws. That man was entirely too handsy for my comfort.

There was a knock at my bedroom door.

Trying to hide seething rage at the world under a tight smile, I strode across the room and opened the door.

A dream stared back at me. Long, midnight black hair, sparkling black eyes, an all-knowing smile...

---

[31] Have I mentioned I was a strange child? I was a strange child. I'd thought up battle plans for those four by the time I was ten. It hadn't helped my parents though, so maybe my strategy needed revision.

"Mempha?" I blinked, trying to sync the image of my imaginary childhood friend with the person standing in front of me wearing a slouchy gray sweatshirt with a tech logo on it, a dark purple bucket hat, and matching sweatpants.

"Wysha?" She tilted her head. "You look like Wysha from the book. Very fey."

"My mother's middle name was Wysh, from the street the hospital was on." It was a nonsensical reply but it was all I had. Someone I'd daydreamed about as a child, written as a teen, and agonized over as an adult was standing in the doorway of my rental bedroom in the wilds of northern California. The whole situation was nonsensical.

And yet...

"You look familiar," I said. "Do I know you?"

"Most people do," the woman agreed. Her English had an accent that I placed as British, but not quite. Hong Kong maybe. "I'm Angel Xi. I play Mempha on the TV show based on the books you wrote. That was you, wasn't it?"

"Yes..." I blinked as latent honesty kicked in. "I mean, my father and I wrote them together. My mother added bits to the first book. That's why we used the author name P.H. Davide. Phoebe, Hayley, and David. Mom's and my middle names were characters—Mempha and Wysha—so we threw my father's middle initial onto the end of his name." I shook my head. "How did you find me?"

"Um, geolocating, bribes, and some blackmail, actually." Angel nodded as she thought about this, clearly willing to give a full accounting and seemingly more worried about the accuracy than the confessions to things I was almost certain were crimes.

"Did anyone answer the door downstairs?

"No."

"But you came in anyway? What if I wasn't here? What if you were wrong?"

Perfectly sculpted eyebrows raised in elegant surprise. "I'm Angel Xi. If I walk into a random house, the people usually trip over themselves to welcome me. If this was the wrong house I'd lie, and then leave after signing autographs."

"That sounds like a good way to get hurt."

"I do my own stunts and have black belts in more than one martial art. Also, I have bear spray with me. Someone recommended it to me when I was renting the car because I said I was going to the mountains. I assume anything that can slow a grizzly down will keep a human at bay too."

"Phoebe?" Adam's voice floated up from downstairs. "There's an extra car outside. Are you okay?"

"Come on up!" I called over Angel's shoulder. "We have a guest."

Adam's familiar footsteps sounded on the stairs and he appeared on the landing like an avenging angel. Except there was already one angel in the room, so maybe he was a devil? A demon? It didn't matter. He appeared wearing a faded green Bigfoot shirt, artfully ripped jeans, and with bare feet.[32] "Hi." He frowned suspiciously at Angel. "You are...?"

"Angel Xi." She tossed her hair, smiled brightly, and looked exactly like someone you wanted to give a million dollars to to do that on camera.

"Right." Adam slipped past her to come stand by me. "Did you invite her?" he asked me.

"No."

"I invited myself." Angel smiled. "I need Phoebe's help."

"To do what?" Offhand I couldn't think of anything I could do that a woman who could find me in Fort Dick, California, based on a couple of videos from a convention and a well-placed bribe or three couldn't do on her own.

---

[32] Yes, they were big. And, yes, I did make a mental note of it in case there was a need for that information later.

For the first time since she'd stormed the barriers, Angel Xi looked nervous. "I want to direct."

I shrugged. "Okay. So, tell someone who can make you a director? I'm not involved at all."

"You know how the series ends," Angel said. "I don't think Mempha winds up with Val."

"No, Mempha winds up ruling. Val dies."[33]

"And Wysha?"

"Winds up with Zjarr Aabo, the cursed dragon."

"What?" Adam sounded horrified and looked ecstatic, which was an odd combo. "Seriously? I thought Z-Wysh was a fever dream! They're endgame?"

The little fandom of two in front of me were both grinning maniacally.

"Yes," I said. "The missing queen was my mom and Val was my dad. We made the story for my mom when she was in the hospital. Eventually, they'd have a happy reunion. But with the queen missing for good, Zjarr and Wysha make the most sense as the happily-ever-after couple because she mirrored the queen, but lived, and in living saves Zjarr from his curse. He loves her in both aspects, and so she loves him too."

"Taeyong-ah[34] is going to be so happy," Angel whispered as she clapped her hands.

"Who?" I didn't know that name.

"Max Kang, he plays Zjarr," Angel explained, waving away further questions. "He kidnapped Iris, the actress who plays Wysha, so they could have a holiday romance away from the city. He's madly in love with her."

Adam frowned. "Does Iris like him back? I thought she

---

[33] Spoiler Alert? Sorry, not sorry.

[34] -ah is a Korean suffix that suggests familiarity or closeness. The -ssi (pronounced *she*) suffix is an all-purpose, gender neutral suffix that shows respect. Korean was not one of the languages I knew before this adventure, but I picked it up.

had a thing going on with the guy playing Val. Well, I did until I saw him in Vegas with a Jpop singer on Everi1."

There was a whole world of internet gossip I was missing. I clapped my hands together. "Focus! Angel Xi, what does this have to do with me?"

"Right." Angel beamed at me and I could see why she got paid a lot of money to smile at cameras. "The fans are voting. Right now, they're voting because they're angry at Iris, not because the story would make sense that way. If you get online and tell Iris what you want, and we record that, the fans will see it. They'll know what ending to vote for.

"Then I get to direct because Mempha has less screen-time. Iris and Taeyong-ah will get to spend more time together. You'll get the promo you need for the books."

"I have plenty of promo," I said dryly. "So much I'm about to throw the last two into a wildfire. Or, well, I was. Adam has convinced me that maybe people aren't as terrible as I remember."

Adam and Angel grimaced in unison and made little seesawing hand motions that suggested I wasn't the only person who found the rest of humanity trying at times.

"The fans will want the real ending," Angel insisted. "Especially since Iris is getting ready to announce to the world that she and Taeyong-ah are more than friends." She typed something into her phone and turned it to show me the screen.

There was a series of pictures showing a fey woman with dark brown hair and fair skin wearing a sunset-purple sweater and a sheer, frilly collar that looked like the hint of a poisonous—at least in the book series—flower. With the pearl-white skirt, the look was a nod to Wysha's more scandalous costumes without being out of place in the modern world. In every picture, her attention seemed to be off-camera. Watching something.

Or someone.

Other pictures showed the rest of the room, a crowd of party-goers and a stunningly beautiful man with black hair, heavy eyebrows, and whose dark eyes were locked across the room. Yes, that was definitely Max Kang, the actor who played my Zjarr Aabo.

A notification appeared with a new picture of the two of them close to each other, looking a breath away from kissing.

"How real is this?" I asked, handing Angel back her phone.

"As real as it comes," she confirmed with a smirk. "Now that everyone knows Jihun-ah is with JSlay,[35] Iris and Taeyong-ah can be together. If the fans ship Iris-ssi and Taeyong-ah, they'll ship Z-Wysh. Ending eight is Z-Wysh. Your book is Z-Wysh. All the stars have aligned. All I need is for the fans to *realize* the stars have aligned so they'll vote for the ending I want."

There was only one small problem there. "That's the ending the studios *don't* want. They've asked me to hold the release of the series so they can have the ending they want."

"The studio wants whatever will make them money," Angel argued. "If the fans change their minds, the studio will agree with them."

"That sounds lovely." Except thinking about it made it hard to breathe.

Angel smiled like I'd just made her Dread Empress of All the Oceans.[36]

"Can I think about it for a minute?"

"Sure!" Angel beamed. "I'll call Iris. We'll do a livestream. The whole fandom is buzzing about the party

---

[35] A Japanese rapper. You may not have heard him, but you've definitely seen his posters. Think about it. Think about it... Yes! *Those* ones. If he was here I'm sure he'd say you're welcome.

[36] Yes, that is a specific reference to a short story. Yes, you should read it.

photos. By the time the studio wakes up, the whole world will be on our side!" She was dialing as she walked away, shutting the door to my bedroom with me and Adam inside.

I looked up at him. "What do I do?"

"About?"

"If this happens, I'm going back to my real life. Back to the spotlight. Back to"—I waved my hand and somehow landed my palm on his—"everything."

"Is that bad?"

"It means I want things. If I want things, I can lose things that matter to me. Lose people that matter."

Adam shrugged as he covered my hand with his free one. "Happiness is the price of sorrow, I guess?"

I mouthed the words and shook my head, anger replacing fear. "What? That makes no sense! Shouldn't sorrow be the price of happiness?"

"Either way, I suppose. You can't have one without the other. If you have everything handed to you in life, it'll never make you happy, because it's your baseline. It's just life. It won't spark joy because it's neutral.

"If you always lose everything you want, then you're simply sad. There's no joy. So you can have neutral and pain without joy, but you can't have joy without the other two. Joy comes from having more of a thing, or an emotion, or time, or whatever, than neutral or bad. So sorrow is the price of happiness."

If I wanted happiness, it sounded like I needed to pursue it. Wanting things could lead to indescribable pain, but it was also the only door to happiness.

How annoying.

I promised myself that if I ever got a chance to re-order the universe, I'd build it differently. But, since I was stuck in a mortal, unmagical form,[37] I was going to choose happiness. I was going to try.

"What if I fail?" I asked Adam as I paced through my room, waiting for Angel Xi to return.

"What if you succeed?"

We shared a look.

"I don't like the mathematics of the coin flip."

He shrugged broad shoulders. "Sorry, Sunshine. Not my department."

"What is your department?" I asked as I took a seat in the highbacked chair near the window.

"What do you want me to be in charge of?" Spring-green eyes met mine and I almost told him the truth. I almost asked him to stay with me.

But Angel walked in, holding her phone and talking to someone. "It's time for you to meet the reason you met me, the author of *All These Broken Seasons*, Phoebe King."

As Angel turned the phone screen to face me, I saw a face that reminded me of my mother. Soft, dark brown hair and limpid brown eyes with a pert nose and a know-

---

[37] Curse all my ancestors for not being mythical creatures.

ing smirk of a smile. Iris Muhly, even without her wig, was everything I'd ever wanted Wysha to be, and more.

"We're recording in three, two, one." Angel waved in front of the camera. "Iris-ssi, say hi."

"Hi," Iris had a voice made for old-time radio, well-rounded and ever-so-slightly exotic.

I nodded to her, trying not to let any of my emotions show. "Hello, it's a pleasure to finally meet you."

"Likewise. Um…" She laughed as she looked around for something. "Line?"

Angel stepped forward so she was in frame. "Iris-ssi, do you like playing Wysha?"

"Of course!" Iris gushed. "Wysha is fantastic. I really relate to how out of place she feels, and how she feels she has no control over anything in her life."

"Wysha isn't going to be weak forever," I said. "In fact, she becomes quite important in the fifth book. And the sixth." I looked over at Adam for support.

He gave me a thumbs up.

"Sixth?" Iris's voice rose an octave in excitement. "I thought there were only five planned."

"We wrote a fifth," I said, "and then, things happened." I glanced at Adam again.

"Good things," he said in a soft rumble that the mic probably didn't pick up.

I nodded, and turned my attention back to Iris, and our audience, with a smile. "I'm back now. The books are already with my publisher. I would like to see them join the *Shattered* series. However, I understand the fans are voting. If they vote for a season five that does not align with the books, I will graciously step aside and allow the series to finish before releasing the final two books for publication."

"And," Iris asked, almost breathless, "if the fans vote for an ending that matches the books?"

"Seeing as the directors have worked hard to be faithful to the titles up to this point, I will, naturally, work with them to ensure the final seasons are up to the excellent standard they've set." My smile was sharp but honest.

"Which ending do you think would result in two more seasons of *Shattered*?"

"Ending eight."

Angel clicked the button to end the livestream as tears welled up in Iris's eyes.

"Ending eight?" she asked breathlessly. "Z-Wysh lives?"

"Z-Wysh lives," I confirmed. "It's the only logical progression for their character arc. The ray of sharp sunshine and the grumpy, overpowered monster who only wants to be loved."

I fought not to look at Adam, and I lost.

From his smile, I guessed he knew exactly what I was thinking.

"This is amazing!" Iris said. "I have to go tell Taeyong-ssi!"

"It is amazing," I agreed.

After all, I'd asked for a sign, and the universe had delivered.

An hour after Angel Xi had swept into my life like a hurricane, I saw her to the door and waved as she drove off.

Tiny snowflakes drifted down from the midnight sky overhead. The cottage's fairyland lights twinkled. "That was possibly the most chaotic hour of my life."

Saying it out loud helped make it real somehow. I thought it would help my racing heart too, but it wasn't fear driving my thoughts, it was excitement.

I could see all the possibilities. With the actors on my side, the people with the star power who could sway the fans, I could see my imaginary world in real life. I could meet the people who had been more of a family to me than anyone alive.

"That was wild," I repeated, because Adam was standing in the foyer looking mildly bemused. "Wasn't it? Angel Xi is on every *Thirty Under 30* list out there. One of the most beautiful women in the world. And she showed up at our rental cottage. That feels like a fever dream." It was amazing what a thirty-second internet search could do for you.

"Pretty sure it actually happened though."

"Pretty sure it means my plans to go back to the mountains are on hold."

"Are you all right with that?"

Taking a breath, I checked in with myself, testing the idea in my head. "Yeah. I think so. It'll be a lot of work, especially if we're publishing the books in tandem with the new season. It'll be a rush. Lots of editing. Angel talked about having me on set to consult with the team on key scenes. So, not quite as laid back as life has been, but it won't be bad."

"Could be fun," Adam said.

"Could be." I looked at him again and I tried to picture an Adam-sized hole next to me as I dove back into the real world. I didn't like the idea. My gaze floated upwards, looking for answers.

And stuck on a ball of festively painted mistletoe.

"Were you aware you were standing under a hemiparasitic plant?" I asked.

"Nooo..." He looked up.

"They're obligate parasites—well, hemiparasites. They can photosynthesize, but they also need the nutrients of the tree they attach to. Take them off it and force them to live on just sunlight, and they die. For the life of me I can't imagine why they're meant to be romantic." Although I did have a good idea why I was rambling.

Adam shrugged. "Every living thing needs support, I guess?"

"Mmm." I took a small step closer. "Are you going to *stay* under the mistletoe?"

"I don't know," his voice dropped, seductive and deep. "Will you climb me like a tree if I do?"

I took another step closer. "Do you want to be climbed like a tree? I might wind up being somewhat hemiparasitic myself. What if I don't want to climb off you later?"

"Don't threaten me with a good time, Sunshine." He held out a hand for me.

I took it and stepped into his embrace. "Um, just so we're very clear, I'm not going to magically become nice or docile or gentle because you kiss me."

Adam nodded, his lips tugging into a smile. "I figured that out already."

"I have no good qualities."

"That's debatable." He hugged me closer. "You're an acquired taste, but I've grown fond of you."

"Really? When?" I rested my hands on his chest. Good knight in a basket, the man really was tall. He must be part redwood.

"I think it started when you stole the starter to my truck and declared yourself my problem."

"I'm not apologizing. That was an excellent decision on my part."

"It was," he agreed. "But, what really sealed it was the fact that you remembered me in the morning. I told you: most people don't. They don't see me."

I raised an eyebrow.

"It's true. You know the safe baby box I told you I was dropped in?"

"Yeah."

"I came with a note saying my mom was checking herself into a mental health hospital. She kept forgetting I was there. She'd walk past the nursery or leave the house and forget I existed."

"Postpartum depression, maybe?"

"Not when it happened to foster families and teachers too. I can walk through crowds unnoticed. I can be forgotten by anyone."

I rested my cheek on his chest, listening to his heartbeat. "Are you worried I'll forget you?"

"A little," he admitted quietly. "I was born a cryptid to everyone around me. I'm as real as Bigfoot. People see me when they need me, or if they want me. But the moment I'm not at the top of their thoughts, I vanish. Every day I've woken up expecting you to forget that I even exist. Every day…" He shrugged.

"Every day you're worried I'll forget I love you?" My heart broke a little at the thought. "Would it be easier to just… stay friends?"

I wanted more.

For the first time in my life, I wanted more. I was willing to work for my happiness. And I wanted Adam with me.

But I could understand why he wouldn't want to risk being abandoned again.

His fingers touched my cheek. "Life is impermanent. Things change. People come and go. If you never take risks because you're afraid of losing, you'll never win anything. You might forget me. You might decide I'm not worth your time. But, right now, you remember me, and I want to spend as much time with you as I can."

"What?" My train of thought completely derailed. "Where did you get that from?"

"A grad school lecture on philosophy and emotional evolution."

I pushed away and looked up in exasperation. "How many university classes did you sit in on?"

"A lot!"

"I can see that!"

"I did get a perfect score on the human anatomy final."

"Oh?"

The corner of his mouth lifted into a wicked grin. "*O* is exactly what I had in mind."

His kiss was warm and wild. His arms tightened as he lifted me up so I could wrap my legs around him. He was perfect, and he was mine.

My fingertips walked across Adam's bare back as I went to trace another Bigfoot tattoo. A week of hiding in the mountain cottage had given me plenty of time to find them all,[38] but I still hadn't picked a favorite.

"That tickles," he murmured into his pillow.

"You should have gotten tattooed somewhere less ticklish."

A heavy arm rose from the mess of blankets and suddenly I was under Adam. Warm, cozy, and smiling under Adam.

He pressed his nose to mine. "You are a menace."

"Your menace," I assured him with a smile.

"Indeed." He lowered himself down to his forearms and started nibbling at my neck.

The phone rang.

Not my ringtone that was a straight-out-of-the-box jingle, but a siren alarm.

Adam rolled off me and grabbed it. "Sandlake."

There was a strident voice on the other end.

Adam's expression darkened as his lips caressed an earthy curse. His eyes met mine.

Trouble? I mouthed.

He nodded.

I moved so he could sit up.

---

[38] Actually, it had taken less than an hour the first night I had Adam naked.

He made a writing motion and I grabbed a pen and paper from the nightstand by his bed. It was the cottage's stationary, but it would work.

As Adam scribbled down numbers, I went to find clothes and hot cocoa.

Ten minutes later, Adam met me in the kitchen, fully dressed and face stern.

"What happened?"

"One of the volunteer fire crews is lost in the backcountry."

"Lost?" I tried not to sound skeptical. "How? I thought the fires were over. There's been rain."

"And the bridge they were using washed out. They went another way, but fire control lost contact with them yesterday. Everyone figured they would be in contact by this morning, but they aren't. There's still patches of fire, reception is spotty out there, and they know at least one guy has an injured ankle. They need someone who knows the area."

"So they remembered you." I nodded in understanding.

Adam shrugged. "That's how it works. In an emergency, people remember me. Any other time, I fade into the background and no one really believes I'm there."

"Being Bigfoot gives you the most useless superpower."

"Helps in crowds though," he said with a sad smile.

"That it does." I sighed and looked down at the whipped cream melting into my cup. "So."

"So."

"You've got to go." I nodded and looked back at him. "You've got to save them. But I'm not going with."

"I wouldn't want you to." The joy that had been in his beautiful green eyes faded with every heartbeat. "It's not safe and this is not going to be a fun trip."

I nodded in understanding. "Got it. I'll be packed in fifteen. You can drop me off anywhere with a car rental.

I'll take it from there."

Our holiday was over. The real world was calling.

"I'm sorry," Adam said. He pulled me close, the way he had a hundred times this week, and kissed the top of my head. "I'm so sorry."

"Do you know how long it will take?"

"A day at least, just to get up there and get in. If I find them right away, it'll still take most of the week to sort out. They'll need me for a bit more."

I nodded slowly, calculating the odds. "Okay. Two weeks from now, there's a thing for the vote. Down in L.A. I'm supposed to go. I want you to be my plus one."

"You mentioned it." Adam hesitated. "It's just..." He looked at the floor.

"It's in two weeks," I said. "And I might forget you exist."

He lifted a shoulder and dropped it in a shrug. "It's not you. It's just how my life is. I'm forgettable."

"I'm not forgetting you," I promised. "I refuse to. I will have your ticket and meet you there if you can't get away earlier. I will be waiting for you."

Green eyes filled with sorrow met mine. "Phoebe, it's—"

"Don't you dare say it's okay if I forget. Don't you dare."

He pressed his lips together, swallowing the excuse.

"I will be there. You will find a way to get there. We will have a date. We will survive the final vote and the fallout thereof."

"Thereof?"

"Don't interrupt. I'm monologuing."

He snickered.

I glared at him. "Our children are going to be absolute monsters. Feral hellions."

"Children?" Adam's face went white with shock.

"Well, not immediately, of course. We've only just started exploring this." I waved a hand between the two of us. "But, eventually, yes. Children. I want a big family and a noisy household. I want to be around people who know me and love me. I want to matter to someone."

Adam blinked and the silence stretched until we could hear the pine trees creaking in the wind outside.

"I did warn you when we first met that you should have left me," I said. "You saved my life and that remains entirely a You Problem."

Adam covered his eyes and sighed. "Listen, Sunshine." He looked at me. "If you remember me in two weeks, you can stay my problem for the rest of my life."

"Good." I nodded. "I'll bring the rings and the prenup. You just have to show up."

"Are you proposing to me?" He laughed.

I glared. "Yes! What else do you expect from this scenario? Do I seem at all like a person who knows how to share?"

"I love you." His eyes regained some of their sparkle as he leaned down to kiss me. "You have all the subtlety of a jackhammer, but I love you."

"If you wanted meek and mild you should have rescued someone else." I stood on tiptoe to kiss his cheek. "There's hot cocoa for you in the microwave. I'll go get packed."

A cold fear settled in my belly, but I kept my smile firmly in place. There was a chance I could lose Adam.

That was fine. People died. I hadn't been able to track down an immortal, so I had to face the reality that Death and I would be fighting each other for someone I loved again at some point.

But even worse was the fear I would forget Adam. That he'd fade from my memory like the cryptid he was.

Everyone else in his life had forgotten him.

...That was fine.

I'd never gone with the crowd before in my life. I wasn't going to start now.

A warm breeze played across the palm trees outside the Peacock Theater in Los Angeles as the crowd sang along to *Shattered's* hit theme song.

The vote had come in and Angel's cunning plan had done the trick.[39] We had the ending I wanted, the one that aligned with the books, and to celebrate, the west coast production team was showing the extended version of last season's finale.[40] Fans paid hundreds for tickets. Those who didn't get in were camped outside. Celebrity fans were walking the red carpet. I'd counted a dozen or so well-known actors at a glance, which was new for me.

Several of them had recognized me, which was stranger still.

And yet… I felt I was forgetting something.

I had a bra on, my dress was an off-the-shoulder A-line dress with a sweetheart neckline in a deep summer-green silk and all the tiny, hand appliqued gems were still on it. My purse was a tiny green clutch barely big enough to fit my phone, newly acquired driver's license, and a bank card.

The ringer was off. My shoes were on. I'd had dinner and managed to locate the VIP snack bar inside after walking the red carpet.

---

[39] And, apparently, wound up with the World's Sexist Villain engaged to the show's Rising Star, much to the delight of the Z-Wysh shippers everywhere.
[40] With bonus scenes I was told were rushed to film between the January 1st New Year and the Lunar New Year.

I'd smiled and posed just like the team taught me.

Still, there was a gnawing sensation that something was wrong. I was supposed to talk to someone. Or see someone. Or tell someone... something.

Hiding in a corner between the bathrooms and the snack bar, I trawled through Everi1 looking for some hint. The headlines tagging me were all either about tonight's event and the new seasons of *Shattered*, or the ongoing dissection of Jack's lies.

Having the stars from the show defend me had changed the way the world viewed the liar taking credit for my work. Was that fair? No, not really. I should have had the acclaim from the get-go, but, like my therapist said, I couldn't change the past. All I could do was make myself a better future.

Skipping past all the speculations about the new season, I went through my checklist.

Had I posted a picture for fans? Yes.

Had I blocked Jack's latest semi-apologetic account? Yes.

Had I—

"Phoebe!" a semi-familiar voice called from behind me.

Frowning, I turned to see a man in a dandelion-yellow suit and a dark blue tie waving at me from the end of the hall.

Ugh. Jack.

"Phoebe!" Jack waved his phone at me. "You blocked me!"

"Yes." Running wasn't really an option, so I stood there and watched him approach with a sinking wave of despair. Some people just did not know how to take a hint.

He stopped just out of reach if I wanted to get a solid punch in, which showed some intelligence at least.[41]

---

[41] I'd been beginning to wonder.

"You blocked me!" Jack repeated.

"Several times," I said flatly. "I thought you'd get the hint that I didn't want to talk to you."

Jack's jaw dropped as his face flushed red. "Don't want—" He stomped his foot and turned to the side, took a breath, and turned back to me. "Why would you not want to talk to me?"

"You mean, aside from the obvious reason that I don't know you and I don't really want to? No," I held up a hand to forestall an argument, "I know that's too complicated for you to understand. Let me make it simple: you tried to steal credit for my work. You vilified me, talked to down to me, and treated me like a simpleton because I don't have a penis and you do. Your entire argument is that you have a higher testosterone level than I do and that makes you a better creative mind.

"But the truth is: I wrote the books. I created the world behind *All These Broken Seasons*. I dreamed up the characters. I. Did. The. Work." I accented each word with a finger stabbing the air. "You didn't."

His face flushed a brighter red. "I could have!"

"Sure." I shrugged. "You could go write your own books. You could create your own worlds. You had that option, and instead you took credit for my work. My worlds. My creations. Why?" I'd never really understood that part. "Why not just make your own?"

"Because I love your world!" Tears shimmered in Jack's eyes. "I wanted to be with Val, and Mempha, and Wysha, and Adamas! They're special! I love them!"

"So do I! So do a lot of people! That doesn't mean you get to claim them as your own."

"Yes it does!"

I sighed. "That's the problem, really," I pointed out. "You think love means ownership. It doesn't. Ownership isn't love. It can't be love. Because love means supporting growth and change and differences.

"You want to own my fictional universe. You want to control it. You want to freeze it forever in a little a box so you can display it on a shelf. That would be fine if it were a painting or a… a rock. But it's a fictional world that lives in my head, so you're trying to capture me and put me on display. You want to control me and you can't, because I'm a living, breathing, changing human being. The only person you can control here is yourself, and you don't want to do that."

Jack blinked at me.

I shrugged again. "I can't change you," I said. "But that doesn't mean I need to let you into my life. You can go and pout, and rage, and want to control things all you want. It's your life. But you don't get to come into my space to pout at me, or rage at me, or demand control of the things in my life. That's not how this works."

"But…" His mouth opened and closed in frustration with nothing coming out but angry huffs. "But, don't you care?"

"About you?" I shook my head. "No. I mean, if you were hit by a car I'd probably stop and call an ambulance for you, but unless you're in immediate danger, no. You're not part of my life. Stop trying to contact me. Go live your own life. I'm going to go live mine." Turning away, I headed towards a display of sets from the TV show, leaving Jack gaping in my wake.

Now, where was I? Had I responded to the video from Iris? Ye—Wait… No!

Dang it. I needed a place to pose.

There was a photo booth down the other side of the wall that had backgrounds from the show. Since most of the celebrity guests were still doing red carpet meet 'n' greets, the photo areas were relatively quiet. I snuck into the line, waited a few minutes, and then took a seat in the infamous forest glen where Zjarr first hinted that he felt anything other than disdain for Wysha.

I'd pictured aspen trees with white bark and golden autumn leaves when I first envisioned the glen. In edits we realized it was springtime. And on camera the aspens became gem-encrusted trees with crystalline trunks and shimmering green leaves.

Rainbows fractured around me as I sat in the filtered spotlight. I pulled up the Everi1 app and posed for pictures, then tagged Iris in them with the caption, "Thinking of you!"

In a few weeks I was going to fly out for the table reading.

A month ago, I'd been safely in my cabin in the mountain, isolated from everyone.

If this was what a month could do, what would a year do?

As if on cue, a sound made me look up into the greenest eyes in the world. The man in front of me wore a tailored blue suit so dark it faded to gray in the shadows. His usually shaggy brown hair had been trimmed into a classic cut, and almost everyone did a double-take as he walked past.

Most of them had the decency to stop looking when they saw the bronze tungsten and redwood ring on his left hand. The rest of them walked past when they saw my glare.

I smiled. "Did you find our seats?"

"Yup. It was the second staircase. We'd gone the wrong way." Adam held out a hand to help me up. "What were you doing?"

"Sending pictures to Iris." Even in heels I had to stand on tiptoe to kiss his cheek. "Are we ready to go up, or do we need to make the rounds still?"

Adam twisted the ring on his finger nervously.

"What's wrong?"

"One of the photographers stopped me."

I blinked, trying to fathom why Adam would be bothered. "Did the picture not turn out?"

"No, I look fabulous." Adam ducked his chin, cheeks turning red. "The photographer told me I was gorgeous."

"Yes." I nodded. "You are."

His smile was soft. "From you, I get that. But having anyone else see me."

"Oh? Are you sad you lost your superpower?"

"It's this ring!" Adam insisted for the third time today. "It's the opposite of the One Ring of Sauron. I put it on, and suddenly I'm visible to everyone! I bet if I take it off I could walk the red carpet unnoticed."

"Babes," I said as I adjusted his tux jacket, "I do not know how to break this to you, but we're in L.A. Not Oregon. The national sport of California is cryptid hunting. Actors. Singers. Anyone wearing their natural hair color. They're all going to be able to see you."

"Thanks, Sunshine. That makes it so much easier to blend in."

"You don't blend in. You only need to be yourself." I kissed his cheek—"I love you."—and took his arm and headed for the photo gauntlet between us and the rest of our quiet[42] evening.

Adam fell in beside me with the hint of a smile curling his delicious lips. "So, this is what it's like being seen. How do people handle it all the time?"

"Most of them don't," I said as we walked down the prep hall to the red carpet area. Already I could hear the chatter of voices in a dozen languages and the whir of digital cameras. "Most people shrink themselves to avoid the edges of their comfort zone. In doing so, they make their comfort zones smaller and smaller until anything new is scary."

---

[42] -ish

"Your therapist told you this?"

"Well," I shrugged, "some of it's therapy and some of it's my own thoughts. I know how easy it was to step away from everything, to give up on everyone—including myself—because anything new hurt."

We stopped in the shadowed archway of the red carpet. Up ahead various celebrities and showrunners waved and smiled at a truly dizzying amount of cameras and the hordes of fans on the bleachers beyond them.

"This is not where I expected to be six months ago," I muttered.

"It's not where I expected to be six weeks ago," Adam muttered back. He squeezed my hand. "We ready for this?"

"We sure are. Let's go dazzle 'em!"

With a wink for him and a smile for the crowd, I stepped into the spotlights.

Life wasn't perfect, it never would be. Life was meant to be messy, hectic, full of ups and downs. There were going to be bad days and good days. There were going to be times I wanted to scream and slam the door on the world, and then there were going to be days like this, where the whole world smiled at me.

That's how life was. Like a line on the hospital monitor, there were ups and downs with every heartbeat. The ever-changing moments, filled with joy and pain, were what showed us we were alive.

As long as I remembered that, I could do anything.

ABOUT THE AUTHOR

IF YOU ASK, LIANA BROOKS WILL TELL YOU SHE HAS A VERY ordinary life. Her daily routines include driving kids to school, cooking meals, writing books, and reading. Truly, all very ordinary things.

If you ask about the scars on her hands, Liana will happily tell you about the moray eel named Baby who bit her while she was hand feeding it for a lab experiment, or about the bite marks from a small shark while she was diving off the coast of California, or a very vicious basketball game. Those stories are all true too.

If you ask where she lives, Liana might say Florida, Alaska, California, South Carolina, or Seoul in the Republic of Korea (South Korea, for the Americans). And she has lived in all those places.

If you ask her about her books, she'll tell you they're all wonderful. And they are! The *Fleet of Malik* books are perfect for readers who want a series of connected sci-fi romances about rebuilding after a decades long war. If it's the enemies-to-lovers trope you're after, try the superhero series *Heroes and Villains*. The *Time and Shadows* time-travel murder mysteries are wonderful for anyone more interested in a body count and crime than romance (though there's a bit of that as well). And the *All I Want For Christmas* series is an excellent escape into holiday romances that don't involve loving Christmases, moving to a small town, or giving up on your dreams.

You can find out more about Liana at her website, www.lianabrooks.com.

MORE BY LIANA BROOKS

Who needs kisses when you could have a werewolf?

Available from all major retailers.

ALL I WANT FOR CHRISTMAS IS A WEREWOLF

THERE WAS MISTLETOE OVER MY DESK. HONEST TO GOODNESS mistletoe hanging over the remains of my Halloween festivities. The Great Pumpkin was now overshadowed by a hemiparasitic shrub.

When I'd left for a conference two hours ago, my desk had been a bastion against the winter holidays. A snow-free island in an otherwise elegantly decorated office suite dedicated to art.

The gallery's front foyer with the dark wood paneling and over-stuffed pine-green tub chairs was now displaying glass-and-metal snowflakes in dazzling designs.

The main negotiating room, with the long table suitable for a fleet of lawyers, had a festive Seasons Greetings banner with pine trees and bright red birds signed by various Miami athletes.

The hall had garlands, multi-colored lights, and occasionally holiday music blaring out of incautiously opened offices.

But this?

This monstrous greenery was not supposed to touch my space.

Elegant Miami's main art gallery across the MacArthur Causeway was a glittering gem of holiday art. But over here, at the offices on Miami Beach that had been selected specifically to be near my boss's favorite house, things were toned down. This was where Elegant Miami hid the nitty gritty details of business. It was the safe space for the sales people that spent all day on the phone with overseas clients; it was the home base of the style teams who went and decorated Miami palaces with carefully curated art from around the world; it was a soulless sovereignty of the contracts office where Maureen and I made sure every jot and tittle were in place.

Tittle was one of my coworker's favorite words. It means the dot over a lower case I or J, but it sounds funny. Stuck in an L-shaped, linoleum-floored concrete bunker with two high windows that looked at the neighboring building a foot away and that always smelled of nail polish and mildew, we took our fun where we could find it.

But I drew the line at plastic Naughty Santa window clings blocking the little sunlight available. Being held hostage by forced holiday cheer was not part of my paycheck.

"Happy holidays, Del!" Maureen jumped out from behind my desk wearing a bright blue sweater with silver bells, dancing elves, and snowflakes. The bell at the end of her bright pink Santa hat with pole dancing elves jingled as she stilled.

I stared, carefully counting to ten in every language I could remember, willing the other half the contracts team to vanish. It wasn't enough. Maureen and her seasonal cheer remained where they were.

"Don't you love it? I'm going to spray some fake snow too!" She pointed around at the sad, red tinsel garlands hanging off the black filing cabinets and the tiny palm tree that was sagging under a strand of rainbow lights.

"That's really not necessary," I said carefully circling around the hazardous airspace of the parasitic plant of unwanted kisses.

What was Maureen even thinking? Who on earth was I going to kiss here? It was against my personal policy to kiss clients or married people. That left Rafael Kane, office grinch, as the only possible target of unwanted contact.

Granted, he was a hot and sexy Office Grinch, but he was also the person voted most likely to ruin a party. He didn't chitchat. He didn't get distracted. He didn't waste time talking to coworkers, going to long Friday lunches, or building friendships.

Rafael Kane went to work, smiled for his clients only, and made Elegant Miami over fifteen percent of our yearly profit. We all loved him for his sales acumen and stunning good looks, but no one around here considered him a friend.

Very early on, I'd tried.

But Rafael Kane had taken one look at me, snarled like I'd stabbed his grandma, and avoided me ever since.

Which suited me just fine.

I frowned. If Maureen thought there was any chance of an office romance, my desk would look like an ad for the Great Bridal Expo. I needed tiny white seed pearls and chiffon as much as I needed mistletoe, which was about as much as a shark needed a tuba.

My idea of a good date was streaming a good murder mystery. I liked crime shows, creepy horror movies, and all things Halloween. People joked that I was a pagan, but that wasn't exactly true. I just loved the idea of magic. It made sense to me.

I should have loved the idea of Santa, except I can't remember a time I wasn't poor, and Santa doesn't visit poor kids.

December was my own personal hell. No winter solstice bonfire would ever be big enough to burn away all my anger at the forced cheer, demand for gifts, and unseasonable expectations.

I wasn't making New Year's Resolutions, I did that on my birthday in July.

I wasn't meeting anyone under the mistletoe, I wasn't that desperate.

I wasn't going to participate in the annual gift exchange, because somehow I always wound up with the bar of soap stolen from the pay-by-the-hour motel down the street.

I would be skipping the party, hitting the white sand beaches of Miami with a pink drink in hand, and spending my three days off catching up on N.W. Gehson's *Serial Killerz* series.

Maureen moved out from behind my desk and pouted. All of five-foot-nothing, she was a cute, apple-shaped woman with sunset pink hair and perpetually purple lips from a permanent makeup choice she made thirty years ago when she was twenty-one, drunk, and planning to be an exotic dancer all her life.[1]

In the bright blue sweater, she looked like the world's glummest Sugar Plum Fairy. She was holding a shiny blue paper with the words "All I Want For The Holidays" and a blank space for a holiday wish on it.

If I ignored the paper, I might escape further holiday interrogations.

"I... I was just trying to be nice!" A huge tear shimmered in her eye.

"I know." I patted her shoulder and tried very hard not to look at the tattoo peeking above her collar that HR insisted she keep covered during work hours. "But I don't like Christmas."

"This year is going to be different!" Maureen assured, her smile turning on like a floodlight in turtle season. "I figured out why you don't like Christmas."

"Because it's a commercial farce to celebrate capitalism?"

"No, silly! Because you're single! No one's giving you the good gifts." She winked and tried to bump me with her

---

[1] She still dances under the name Cotton Candy every other Friday down at the Sugar Strip on 4th, if you're wondering.

hip, but since her head only comes up to my shoulder even in kitten heels, it didn't quite work.

I scooted around her and into my three-sided box of an office.

There were sparkly confetti snowflakes covering the nameplate that had been a gift from one of my favorite metalwork artists.

Delinna Farmer was not a name that deserved to have snow on it. Especially fake snow.

Shaking the snow off the metal cut-out of my name, I smiled up at Maureen. "Really, Maureen, I'm fine."

"You will be!" She pulled a scroll of candy pink paper out of her cleavage so it unrolled in a long, curling list. "This is Auntie Maureen's list of acceptable bachelors in the greater Miami area."

"Maureen," I said, sitting down and giving her my very best glare, "if Rafael Kane is mentioned even once on that list, I will murder you. Right here and now. There will be blood all over your dancing elf sweater. No jury will convict me."

She rolled her eyes. "Tried that. Obviously there's chemistry there, but Rafe could have chemistry with a doorknob, so it doesn't matter." She put the list of names —written in pink and purple ink—on my desk. "Names. Numbers. Histories. Sizes."

"Siz—Oh!" I covered my mouth. "Sweet mother of pearl! Maureen! This is so invasive!" I crumpled the list up and dropped it in the recycling bin.

"A girl's got to know…"

"I do not need to know anyone's sizes!" I shouted as the door to the contracts office opened and the devil himself walked in.

Rafael's brown eyes went wide, his tan face frozen in a rictus of horror.

"I'm not participating in the company Christmas party and I'm not ordering the shirts," I said loudly, willing

Maureen to play along. Rafael might be the office grinch, but nobody gossiped as much as his people in the sales department. If he even guessed at the content of Maureen's list, I'd have every art gallery employee and intern in the greater Miami area sending me extra details.

Maureen, oblivious to the threat of Dick Pic Armageddon, crossed her arms over her ample chest. "Why not? What's wrong with the holiday party?"

"Because..." I scrambled for an excuse that wouldn't insult Maureen's party planning. "...I'm seeing someone."

Rafael snorted in amusement as he shook his head and walked to our copy machine by the door. The sales department had a better one, one that could print posters and banners, but it was broken and the sales associates had been bouncing in and out of the contracts office all week. There was nothing like the holidays to convince the obscenely wealthy to drop hundreds of thousands of dollars on art.

"Oh, sweetie," Maureen said, grabbing my arm and leaning in for a sideways hug as she ignored Rafael. "You don't need to lie."

"I'm not," I lied. "I am in a relationship. And I think it's serious. We're talking about moving in together."

From the copier Rafael gave me a look of disbelief that said, *No one would ever live with you.*

Maureen patted my hand with a tiny sigh of pity. "Let me guess. His name is Nick 'The Closer' Claus and you ordered him from the toys department at Lady Things downtown? I've met him too." Her smile was wicked. "But he doesn't count as a dinner date."

Too. Much. Information.

Closing my eyes, I focused on the filing list I needed to finish today. Anything to get the image of my middle-aged co-worker gleefully bouncing through the adult toy store out of my head.

In my imagination, she wore a frilled pink skirt that barely covered her ample thighs. I shuddered.

My only option was to lie more, or to hope Rafael would step in to help me. "Maureen—"

"No!" Rafael shouted from across the room. "No more. Not until I leave. I do not need to hear this. Let me finish. Please. Five more pages!"

Just for that I wanted to play dirty, but encouraging Maureen would give me a heart attack. There was only one course of action left...

"I'm getting a dog," I said before the dick pics became porno subscriptions in my stocking. "I've been visiting the shelters and I'm planning to adopt one over the holidays."

Maureen's shoulders sagged. "Honey, that does not count."

"A dog will be more loyal than any man will!" I drew myself up, a furious dark queen with a mask of rage perfected after years of studying every campy Halloween vampire movie ever. Morticia Addams, eat your heart out. "Probably more loyal than a woman, too. It'll love me, wait for me, and cuddle with me while I watch horror movies in December. A dog won't make me watch cheesy Christmas specials. A dog will go for walks on the beach with me. A dog will be happy eating whatever I cook—"

"A dog should have a high-protein diet."

Maureen and I both turned to stare.

Had Rafael Kane actually joined a conversation that wasn't about sales? After all these years?

"Do you like dogs?" Maureen asked politely, reverting back to Sweet Office Eccentric like a chameleon. "You've never mentioned them."

Rafael stared at the wall behind the copier as he realized his mistake. His body went rigid and I swear I saw a shiver of terror shimmy through him. He knew Maureen would never let him escape now.

"My mother raised dogs when I was growing up." He finished his copy work and turned to glare at me. "I've seen the stuff you eat for lunch, Del. Do the world a favor and stick to stuffed animals and battery-operated toys. A dog deserves better." He opened his mouth as if he were going to continue, then snapped it shut and marched out, back stiff.

Maureen hummed happily. "He has such a nice tush!"

"Maureen!" I smacked her arm.

"What? I'm married, not dead. I can look."

"We're at work."

"Quitting time was eight minutes ago. I can lust after people off the clock."

"You are a dirty old woman."

"Yes I am," she said proudly.

I rolled my eyes and remembered why I'd come back in. "I need to get my water bottles. I keep forgetting them." Nine of them sat in a row by my spare shoes.

"Oh, is that what happened?" Maureen asked. "I thought you'd decided to decorate with them. Maybe make a shrine to your beloved *agua*."

"Ha ha, funny." I grabbed a big bag with the name of a local farmer's stall on it and stuffed the water bottles inside. "The winter wonderland stuff… Can you keep it off my desk?"

Maureen pouted again.

"Please? I'll bring you some of those spiced pecans you like." If the bodega had a BOGO sale going on. If it wasn't buy-one-get-one, I wasn't sharing.

Her eyes went wide with delight. "Consider it gone. I will leave your corner a natural wasteland of bones, ghouls, and whatever that thing is," she said pointing to my Zany Zombie bobblehead.

"Thank you." I packed up and went home to research animal shelters. If I was going to be forced to participate in the holidays, I deserved to have someone who was happy to see me every day.

Surely I could get a dog for Christmas. It couldn't be that hard.

Keep reading! Head to
www.inkprintpress.com/lianabrooks/christmas/werewolf/
to buy your copy now!

Milton Keynes UK
Ingram Content Group UK Ltd.
UKHW021129271124
3088UKWH00005BA/8

9 781922 434999